COLLECTION 15

COLLECTION 15

How to Kill a Monster
Legend of the Lost Legend
Attack of the Jack-O'-Lanterns

R.L. Stine

Scholastic Children's Books,
Commonwealth House, 1–19 New Oxford Street, London WC1A 1NU, UK
a division of Scholastic Ltd
London ~ New York ~ Toronto ~ Sydney ~ Auckland
Mexico City ~ New Delhi ~ Hong Kong

First published in this edition by Scholastic Ltd, 1999

How to Kill a Monster
Legend of the Lost Legend
Attack of the Jack-O'-Lanterns
First published in the US by Scholastic Inc., 1996
First published in the UK by Scholastic Ltd, 1997

ISBN 0 439 01228 7

Typeset by Rowland Phototypesetting Ltd, Bury St Edmunds, Suffolk
Printed by Cox & Wyman Ltd, Reading, Berks.

10 9 8 7 6 5 4 3 2 1

CONTENTS

1 How to Kill a Monster   1

2 Legend of the Lost Legend   117

3 Attack of the Jack-O'-Lanterns   243

Goosebumps

How to
Kill a Monster

"Why do we have to go there?" I wailed from the back seat of the car. "Why?"

"Gretchen, I've told you three times *why*." Dad sighed. "Your mother and I have to go to Atlanta. For work!"

"I know that," I replied, leaning over the front seat. "But why can't we go with you? Why do we have to stay with Grandma and Grandpa?"

"Because we said so," Mum and Dad declared together.

Because we said so. Once they said those deadly words, there was no use arguing.

I slumped down in my seat.

Mum and Dad had some kind of work emergency in Atlanta. They got the call this morning.

It's not fair, I thought. They get to visit a cool city like Atlanta. And Clark—my stepbrother—and I have to go to Mud Town.

Mud Town.

Well, it's not really called Mud Town. But it

should be. Because it's a swamp. Grandma Rose and Grandpa Eddie live in southern Georgia—in a swamp.

Can you believe it?

A swamp.

I stared out the car window. We'd been riding on highways all day. Now we were driving on a narrow road through the swamp.

It was late afternoon. And the cypress trees began to cast long shadows over the marshy grass.

I stuck my head out the window. A blast of hot, humid air hit my face. I ducked back in and turned to Clark. His nose was buried in a comic book.

Clark is twelve—like me. He's much shorter than I am. Much shorter. And he has curly brown hair, brown eyes, and tons of freckles. He looks exactly like Mum.

I'm quite tall for my age. I have long, straight blonde hair and green eyes. I look like Dad.

My parents divorced when I was two years old. The same thing happened to Clark. My dad and his mum married each other straight after our third birthdays, and we all moved into a new house together.

I like my stepmother. And Clark and I get along okay, I suppose. He acts like a jerk sometimes. Even my friends say so. But I think their brothers act like jerks, too.

I stared at Clark.

Watched him read.

His glasses slid down his nose.

He pushed them up.

"Clark . . ." I started.

"Shhhh." He waved his hand at me. "I'm at the good part."

Clark loves comic books. Scary ones. But he's not brave—so he's always terrified by the time he finishes.

I glanced out the window again.

I stared at the trees. At the branches, all draped in long grey webs. They dangled from every tree—curtains of grey. They made the swamp look really gloomy.

Mum had told me about the grey webs when we were packing this morning. She knows a lot about swamps. She thinks swamps are pretty— in a spooky sort of way.

Mum said the grey webs were actually a swamp plant that grew right on the trees.

A plant that grows on a plant. Weird, I thought. Definitely weird.

Almost as weird as Grandma and Grandpa.

"Dad, how come Grandma and Grandpa never visit us?" I asked. "We haven't seen them since we were four."

"Well, they're a little strange." Dad peered at me through the rear-view mirror. "They don't like to travel. They almost never leave their house. And they live so far back in the swamp, it's very hard to visit them."

"Oh, wow!" I said. "A sleepover with two strange old hermits."

"Smelly, strange old hermits," Clark mumbled, glancing up from his comic.

"Clark! Gretchen!" Mum scolded. "Don't talk about your grandparents that way."

"They're not my grandparents. They're hers." Clark jerked his head towards me. "And they do smell. I can still remember it."

I punched my stepbrother in the arm. But he was right. Grandma and Grandpa did smell. Like a combination of mildew and mothballs.

I sank deep into my seat and let out a loud yawn.

It seemed as if we'd been riding in the car for weeks. And it was really crowded back there— with me, Clark and Charley squished together. Charley is our dog—a golden retriever.

I pushed Charley out of the way and stretched out.

"Quit shoving him on to me!" Clark complained. His comic book dropped to the floor.

"Sit still, Gretchen," Mum muttered. "I knew we should have boarded Charley."

"I tried to find a kennel for him," Dad said. "But no one could take him at the last minute."

Clark pushed Charley off his lap and reached down for his comic. But I grabbed it first.

"Oh, brother," I moaned when I read the title. "*Creatures from the Muck*? How can you read this rubbish?"

"It's not rubbish," Clark shot back. "It's really cool. Better than those stupid nature magazines you read."

"What's it about?" I asked, flipping through the pages.

"It's about some totally gross monsters. Half-human. Half-beast. They set traps to catch people. Then they hide under the mud. Near the surface," Clark explained. He grabbed the comic from my hand.

"Then what happens?" I asked.

"They wait. They wait as long as it takes—for the humans to fall into their traps." Clark's voice started to quiver. "Then they force them deep into the swamp. And make them their slaves!"

Clark shuddered. He glanced out the window. Out at the eerie cypress trees with their long beards of grey.

It was growing dark now. The trees' shadows shifted over the tall grass.

Clark lowered himself in his seat. He has a wild imagination. He really believes the stuff he reads. Then he gets scared—like now.

"Do they do anything else?" I asked. I wanted Clark to tell me more. He was really scaring himself.

7

"Well, at night, the monsters rise up from the mud," he went on, sliding down in his seat some more. "And they drag kids from their beds. They drag them into the swamp. They drag them down into the mud. No one ever sees the kids again. Ever."

Clark was totally freaked now.

"There really are creatures like that in the swamp. I read about them in school," I lied. "Horrible monsters. Half-alligator, half-human. Covered with mud. With spiky scales underneath, hidden. If you just brush against one, the scales rip the flesh right off your bones."

"Gretchen, stop," Mum warned.

Clark hugged Charley close to him.

"Hey! Clark!" I pointed out the window to an old narrow bridge up ahead. Its wooden planks sagged. It looked ready to crumble. "I bet a swamp monster is waiting for us under that bridge."

Clark gazed out the window at the bridge. He hugged Charley closer to him.

Dad began steering the car over the old wooden planks. They rumbled and groaned under the weight.

I held my breath as we slowly rolled across. This bridge can't hold us, I thought. No way.

Dad drove very, very slowly.

It seemed to take for ever to ride across.

8

Clark clung to Charley. He kept his eyes out the window, glued to the bridge.

When we finally neared the end, I let out a long whoosh of air.

And then I gasped—as a deafening explosion rocked the car.

"Nooo!" Clark and I both screamed as the car swerved wildly.

Skidded out of control.

It crashed into the side of the old bridge.

Ploughed right through the old wood.

"We—we're going down!" Dad cried.

I shut my eyes as we plunged into the swamp.

We hit hard, with a loud *thud*.

Clark and Charley bounced all over the back seat. When the car finally slid to a stop, they were sitting on top of me.

"Is everyone okay?" Mum asked in a shaky voice. She turned to the back.

"Uh-huh," I replied. "I think."

We all sat quietly for a moment.

Charley broke the silence with a soft whimper.

"Wh-what happened?" Clark stammered.

"Flat tyre." Dad sighed. "I hope the spare is okay. There's no way we're going to get help at night in the middle of a swamp."

I leaned out the window to check the tyre. Dad was right. It was totally flat.

Boy, were we lucky, I thought. Lucky this was a low bridge. Otherwise . . .

"Okay, everybody out of the car," Mum interrupted my thoughts. "So Dad can change the tyre."

Clark took a long look out the car window before he opened the door. I could tell he was afraid.

"Better be careful, Clark," I said as he swung his short, stubby legs out the door. "The swamp monster likes low targets."

"That's funny, Gretchen. Really funny. Remind me to laugh."

Dad headed for the boot to find the jack. Mum followed. Clark and I stepped into the swamp.

"Oh, gross!" My brand-new white trainers sank into the thick black mud.

I let out a long sigh.

How could anyone live in a swamp? I wanted to know. It was so gross out here.

The air felt thick and soupy. So hot, it was hard to breathe.

As I pulled my hair back into a scrunchie, I glanced around.

I couldn't see much. The sky had darkened to black.

Clark and I drifted away from the car. "Let's explore while Dad fixes the tyre," I suggested.

"I don't think that's such a great idea," Clark murmured.

"Sure it is," I urged. "There's nothing else to do. And it's better than standing around here, waiting. Isn't it?"

"I—I suppose so," Clark stammered.

We took a few steps into the swamp. My face began to tingle and itch.

Mosquitoes! Hundreds of them.

We ducked and dodged, frantically brushing them off our faces, off our bare arms.

"Yuck! It's disgusting out here!" Clark cried. "I'm not staying here. I'm going to Atlanta!"

"It's not this buggy at Grandma's house," Mum called out.

"Oh, sure." Clark rolled his eyes. "I'm going back to the car."

"Come on," I insisted. "Let's just see what's over there." I pointed to a patch of tall grass up ahead.

I stomped through the mud, glancing over my shoulder—to make sure Clark was following me. He was.

As we reached the grass, we could hear a loud rustling deep in the blades. Clark and I peered down, straining to see in the dark.

"Don't wander too far," Dad warned, as he and Mum pulled our luggage from the boot, searching for a torch. "There might be snakes out there."

"Snakes? Whoa!" Clark jumped away. He started running full speed back to the car.

"Don't be a baby!" I called after him. "Let's do some exploring."

"No way!" He choked out the words. "And don't call me a baby."

"I'm sorry," I apologized. "Come on. We'll walk

over to that tree. The one that towers over the others. It's not that far away. Then we'll come right back," I promise. "Puh-lease."

Clark and I started towards the tree.

We walked slowly. Through the darkness. Through the jungle of cypress trees.

The curtains of grey swayed on the tree branches. They were so thick—thick enough to hide behind.

It would be really easy to get lost in here, I realized. Lost for ever.

I shuddered as the heavy grey curtains brushed against my skin. They felt like spider webs. Huge, sticky spider webs.

"Come on, Gretchen. Let's turn back," Clark pleaded. "It's gross out here."

"Just a little further," I urged him on.

We made our way carefully through the trees, sloshing through puddles of inky water.

Tiny insects buzzed in my ears. Bigger ones bit at my neck. I swatted them away.

I stepped forward—on to a dry, grassy patch of ground. "Whoa!"

The patch started to move. Started to float across the black water.

I leaped off—and stumbled on a tree root. No—not a tree root. "Hey, Clark. Look at this!" I bent to get a better look.

"What is *that*?" Clark kneeled beside me and peered at the knobby form.

"It's called a cypress knee," I explained. "Mum told me about them. They grow near the cypress trees. They rise up from the roots."

"How come Mum never tells *me* about these things?" he demanded.

"I suppose she doesn't want to scare you," I replied.

"Yeah, right," he muttered, pushing up his glasses. "Want to go back now?"

"We're almost there. See?" I said, pointing to the tall tree. It stood in a small clearing just a few metres away.

Clark followed me into the clearing.

The air smelled sour here.

The night sounds of the swamp echoed in the darkness. We could hear low moans. Shrill cries. The moans and cries of swamp creatures, I thought. Hidden swamp creatures.

A shiver ran down my spine.

I moved deeper into the clearing. The tree with the high branches stood right before me.

Clark stumbled over a log. Stumbled into a black pool of mucky water.

"That's it," he groaned. "I'm outta here."

Even in the dark, I could see the frightened expression on Clark's face.

It *was* scary in the swamp. But Clark seemed so petrified that I started to giggle.

And then I heard the footsteps.

Clark heard them too.

14

Heavy, thudding footsteps across the black, misty swamp.

Charging closer.

Heading straight for us.

"Come on!" Clark cried, yanking on my arm. "Time to go!"

But I didn't move. I *couldn't* move.

Now I could hear the creature's breathing. Heavy, rasping breaths. Nearer. Nearer.

It came springing out. From behind the grey-bearded tree limbs.

A tall black form. A huge swamp creature. Loping towards us. Darker than the black swamp mud—with glowing red eyes.

"Charley—! What are you doing down there?" Mum cried, marching into the clearing. "I thought you kids were watching him."

Charley?

I'd forgotten all about Charley.

Charley was the swamp monster.

"I've been looking all over for you," Mum snapped angrily. "Didn't we tell you to stay by the car? Dad and I have been searching everywhere."

"Sorry, Mum," I apologized. I couldn't say any more. Charley leaped on me and knocked me down—into the mud.

"Off! Charley! Off!" I shouted. But he planted his huge paws on my shoulders and licked my face.

I was covered in mud. Totally covered.

"Come on, boy." Clark tugged on Charley's collar. "You were scared, Gretchen. You thought

Charley was a swamp monster." Clark laughed. "You were really scared."

"I—I was not," I sputtered, wiping the mud from my jeans. "I was just trying to scare you."

"You were really scared. Just admit it," Clark insisted. "Just admit it."

"I was NOT scared." My voice started to rise. "Who was the one begging to go back?" I reminded him. "You! You! You!"

"What's all the fighting about?" Dad demanded. "And what are you two doing way out here? Didn't I tell you to stay near the car?"

"Um, sorry, Dad," I apologized. "But we were kind of bored, just waiting around."

"We! What do you mean *we*? It was all Gretchen's idea," Clark protested. "She was the one who wanted to explore the swamp."

"That's enough!" Dad scolded. "Everyone— back to the car."

Clark and I argued all the way back. Charley trotted by my side, flinging more mud on my jeans.

The flat tyre had been fixed—but now Dad had to get the car back on the road. And it wasn't easy. Every time he stepped on the accelerator, the tyres just spun around and around in the thick mud.

Finally, we all got out and pushed.

Now Mum and Clark were splattered with mud, too.

As we drove away, I stared out at the dark, eerie marsh.

And listened to the night sounds.

Sharp chitters.

Low moans.

Shrill cries.

I'd heard lots of stories about swamp monsters. And I'd read some ancient legends about them. Could they be real? I wondered. Do swamp monsters really exist?

Little did I know that I would soon find out the answer to that question. The hard way.

"Yes. Yes. They do."

"No way!" I told Dad. "That can't be where they live!"

"That's their house," Dad insisted as the car bumped up a narrow sandy road. "That's Grandma and Grandpa's house."

"That *can't* be their house." Clark rubbed his eyes. "It's a swamp mirage. I read about them in *Creatures from the Muck*. The swamp mud plays tricks on your eyes. It makes you see things."

See what I mean about Clark? He really does believe the stuff he reads.

And it was beginning to sound right to me, too. How else could you explain Grandma and Grandpa's house?

A castle.

A castle in the middle of a swamp.

Almost hidden in a grove of dark, towering trees.

Dad pulled the car up to the front door. I stared at the house in the glow of the headlights.

Three storeys high. Built of dark grey stone. A turret rose up on the right side. On the left, a sliver of white smoke curled from a blackened chimney.

"I thought swamp houses were smaller," I murmured, "and built on stilts."

"That's the way they look in my comic," Clark agreed. "And what's with the windows?" His voice shook. "Are they vampires or something?"

I stared at the windows. They were tiny. And I could see only three of them. Three tiny windows in the entire house. One on each floor.

"Come on, kids," Mum said. "Let's get your luggage."

Mum, Dad and Clark climbed out of the car and headed for the boot. I stood by the car door with Charley.

The night air felt cold and damp on my skin. I stared up.

Up at the big dark house. Almost hidden behind the trees. In the middle of nowhere.

And then I heard the howl. A mournful howl. From somewhere deep in the swamp.

A chill swept through me.

Charley pressed against my leg. I bent to pet him. "What could that be?" I whispered to the dog in the dark. "What kind of creature howls like that?"

"Gretchen. Gretchen." Mum waved from the front door of the house. Everyone else had gone inside.

"Oh, my," Grandma said as I stepped into the dim entrance. "This can't be our little Gretchen." She wrapped her frail arms around me and gave me a big hug.

She smelled just the way I had remembered—musty. I glanced at Clark. He rolled his eyes.

I stepped back and forced a smile.

"Move aside, Rose," Grandpa yelled. "Let me get a look at her."

"He's a little hard-of-hearing," Dad whispered to me.

Grandpa clasped my hand between his wrinkled fingers. He and Grandma seemed so slight. So fragile.

"We're really happy you're here!" Grandma exclaimed. Her blue eyes twinkled. "We don't get many visitors!"

"For a while, we thought you weren't coming!" Grandpa shouted. "We expected you hours ago."

"Flat tyre," Dad explained.

"Tired?" Grandpa wrapped his arms around Dad. "Well, then come in and sit down, son."

Clark giggled. Mum shoved an elbow into his side. Grandpa and Grandma led us into the living room.

The room was enormous. Our whole house could probably fit inside it.

The walls were painted green. Drab green. I stared up at the ceiling. Up at an iron chandelier that held twelve candles, in a circle.

An enormous fireplace took up most of one wall.

The other walls were covered with black-and-white photographs. Yellowed with age.

Photographs everywhere. Of people I didn't recognize. Probably dead relatives, I thought.

I glanced through a doorway into the next room. The dining room. It appeared to be as big as the living room. Just as dark. Just as dreary.

Clark and I sat down on a tattered green couch. I felt the old springs sag under my weight. Charley groaned and stretched out on the floor at our feet.

I glanced around the room. At the pictures. At the worn rug. At the shabby tables and chairs. The flickering light high above us made our shadows dance on the dark walls.

"This place is creepy," Clark whispered. "And it really smells bad—worse than Grandma and Grandpa."

I choked back a laugh. But Clark was right. The room smelled strange. Damp and sour.

Why do two old people want to live like this? I wondered. In this musty, dark house. Deep in the swamp.

"Would anyone like something to drink?"

Grandma interrupted my thoughts. "How about a nice cup of tea?"

Clark and I shook our heads no.

Mum and Dad also said no. They sat opposite us. The stuffing in their chairs spilled out of the backs.

"Well, you're finally here!" Grandpa yelled to us. "It's just great. So, tell me—how come you were late?"

"Grandpa," Grandma shouted to him, "no more questions!" Then she turned to us. "After such a long trip, you must be starving. Come into the kitchen. I made my special chicken pot pie—just for you."

We followed Grandma and Grandpa into the kitchen. It looked like all the other rooms. Dark and dingy.

But it didn't smell as ancient as the other rooms. The tangy aroma of chicken pot pie floated through the air.

Grandma removed eight small pies from the oven. One for each of us—and a couple of extras in case we were starving, I guessed.

Grandma placed one on my plate, and I began to dig right in. I *was* starving.

As I lifted the fork to my mouth, Charley sprang up from his place on the floor and started to sniff.

He sniffed our chairs.

The worktop.

The floor.

He leaped up to the table and sniffed.

"Charley, stop!" Dad ordered. "Down!"

Charley jumped from the table. Then he reared up in front of us—and curled his upper lip

He let out a growl.

A low, menacing growl that erupted into loud barking.

Furious barking.

"What on earth is wrong with him?" Grandma demanded, frowning at the dog.

"I don't know," Dad told her. "He's never done that before."

"What is it, Charley?" I asked. I shoved my chair from the table and approached him.

Charley sniffed the air.

He barked.

He sniffed some more.

A chill of fear washed over me.

"What is it, boy? What do you smell?"

I grabbed Charley's collar. Petted him. Tried to calm him down. But he jerked out of my grasp.

He barked even louder.

I reached for his collar again and tugged him towards me. His nails scraped the floor as he pulled away.

The more I tugged on his collar, the harder Charley fought. He swung his head sharply from side to side. And started to growl.

"Easy, boy," I said softly. "Eeea—sy."

Nothing worked.

Finally Clark helped me drag Charley into the living room—where he started to settle down.

"What do you think is wrong with him?" Clark asked as we stroked the dog's head.

"I don't know." I stared down at Charley. Restless now, he turned in circles. Then he sat. Then turned in circles. Again and again.

"I just don't get it. He's never done that before. Ever."

Clark and I decided to wait in the living room with Charley while Mum and Dad finished eating. We weren't hungry any more.

"How's that dog of yours?" Grandpa came in and sat down next to us. He ran his wrinkled fingers through his thinning grey hair.

"Better," Clark answered, pushing his glasses up.

"Pet her?" Grandpa hollered. "Sure! If you think that will help."

After dinner, Mum, Dad, Grandma and Grandpa talked and talked—about practically everything that had happened since they last saw each other. Eight years ago.

Clark and I were bored. Really bored.

"Can we, um, watch television?" Clark finally asked.

"Oh, sorry, dear," Grandma apologized. "We don't have a television."

Clark glowered at me—as if it was my fault.

"Why don't you call Arnold?" I suggested. Arnold is the biggest nerd in our neighbourhood. And Clark's best friend. "Remind him to pick up your new comic."

"Okay," Clark grumbled. "Um, where's the phone?"

"In town." Grandma smiled weakly. "We don't know many people—still alive. Doesn't pay to have a phone. Mr Donner—at the general store—he takes messages for us."

"Haven't seen Donner all week, though," Grandpa added. "Our car broke down. Should be fixed soon. Any day now."

No television.

No phone.

No car.

In the middle of a swamp.

This time it was my turn to glower—at Mum and Dad.

I put on my angriest face. I was sure they were going to take us to Atlanta with them now. Absolutely sure.

Dad glanced at Mum. He opened his mouth to speak. Then he turned towards me. And shrugged an apology.

"Guess it's time for bed!" Grandpa checked his watch. "You two have to get an early start," he said to Mum and Dad.

"Tomorrow you're going to have so much fun," Grandma assured Clark and me.

"Yes, indeed," Grandpa agreed. "This big old house is great to explore. You'll have a real adventure!"

"And I'm going to bake my famous rhubarb pie!" Grandma exclaimed. "You kids can help me. You'll love it. It's so sweet, your teeth will fall out after one bite!"

I heard Clark gulp.

I groaned—loudly.

Mum and Dad ignored us. They said good night. And goodbye. They were leaving really early in the morning. Probably before we got up.

We followed Grandma up the dark, creaky old steps and down a long, winding hall to our rooms on the first floor.

Clark's room was right next to mine. I didn't have a chance to see what it looked like. After Clark had gone in, Grandma quickly ushered me to my room.

My room. My gloomy room.

I set my suitcase down next to the bed and glanced around. The room was nearly as big as a gym! And it didn't have a single window.

The only light came from a dim yellow bulb in a small lamp next to the bed.

A handmade rug covered the floor. Worn thin in spots, its rings of colour were dingy with age.

A warped wooden dresser sat against the wall opposite the bed. It leaned to one side. The drawers hung out.

A bed. A lamp. A dresser.

Only three pieces of furniture in this huge, windowless room.

Even the walls were bare. Not a single picture covered the dreary grey paint.

I sat down on the bed. I leaned against the bars of the iron headboard.

I ran my fingers over the blanket. Scratchy wool. Scratchy wool that smelled of mothballs.

"There's no way I'm going to use that blanket," I said out loud. "No way." But I knew I would. The room was cold and damp, and I began to shiver.

I quickly changed into my pyjamas and pulled the smelly old blanket over me.

I twisted and turned. Trying to get comfortable on the lumpy mattress.

I stared up at the ceiling and listened. Listened to the night sounds of the creepy old house. Strange creaking noises that echoed through the old walls.

Then I heard the howls.

Frightening animal howls on the other side of the wall.

The sad howls from the swamp.

I sat up.

Were they coming from Clark's room?

I listened hard, afraid to move.

Another long, sad howl. From outside. Not from Clark's room.

"Stop it!" I scolded myself. "Clark is the one with the wild imagination. Not you!"

But I couldn't shut out the eerie howls from the swamp.

Was it an animal? Was it a swamp monster?

I pressed the pillows over my face. It took me hours to fall asleep.

When I woke up, I didn't know if it was morning—or the middle of the night. Without a window, it was impossible to tell.

I read my watch—8:30. Morning.

I searched through the suitcase for my new pink T-shirt. I needed something to cheer me up—and pink is my favourite colour. I pulled on my jeans. Slipped on my muddy trainers.

I dressed quickly. The room reminded me of a prison cell. I wanted to escape fast.

I opened the bedroom door and peeked into the hall.

Empty.

But there, opposite my room, I saw a small window. I hadn't noticed it the night before.

A bright ray of sunshine filtered through the dusty glass. I peered outside—into the swamp.

A heavy mist hung over the red cypress trees, casting a soft, rosy glow over the wet land. The glowing mist made the swamp look mysterious and unreal.

Something purple fluttered on a nearby tree limb. A purple bird. A purple bird with a bright orange beak. I'd never seen a bird like that before.

Then I heard the sounds again.

The horrible howls. The shrill cries.

From animals hiding deep in the swamp— all kinds of creatures I'd probably never seen before.

Swamp creatures.

Swamp monsters.

I shuddered. Then turned away from the window and headed for Clark's room.

I knocked on the door. "Clark!"

No answer.

"Clark?"

Silence.

I burst through the door and let out a cry.

The sheets on Clark's bed lay in a tangled

mess—as if there had been some kind of struggle.

And now there was nothing left of Clark—nothing but part of his pyjamas, crumpled on the bed!

"Noooo!"

I opened my mouth in a terrified cry.

"Gretchen—what's your problem?"

Clark stepped out from the wardrobe.

He wore a T-shirt, baseball cap, trainers and his pyjama bottoms.

"Uh . . . n-no problem," I stammered, my heart still pounding.

"Then why did you scream?" Clark demanded. "And why do you look so weird?"

"*I* look weird? You're the one who looks weird," I snapped. I pointed to his pyjama bottoms. "Where are your trousers?"

"I don't know." He shook his head. "I think Mum must have packed them in your suitcase by mistake."

I have to stop letting this big, old house spook me. Clark is the one with the wild imagination—not me, I reminded myself again.

"Come on," I told my stepbrother. "Let's go back to my room and look for your jeans."

On the way down to breakfast, Clark stopped to peer out of the hall window. The mist had cleared. The dew-covered plants glistened in the sunlight.

"It looks quite pretty, doesn't it?" I murmured.

"Yeah," Clark replied. "Pretty. Pretty creepy."

The kitchen looked pretty creepy too. It was dark—almost as dark in the morning as the night before. But the back door was open and some sun splashed on the floor and the walls.

We could hear the sounds of the swamp through the open door. But I tried to ignore them.

Grandma stood by the stove, a spatula in one hand, a huge plate of blueberry pancakes in the other. She set down the spatula and plate and wiped her hands on her faded flower apron. Then she gave us each a big good-morning hug— smearing Clark with pancake batter.

I pointed at the stains on his shirt and giggled. Then I glanced down at my shirt. My brand-new pink T-shirt. Splotched with blueberry stains.

I glanced around the kitchen for something to use to clean my shirt. The room was a disaster.

Globs of pancake batter dripped from the stove. Batter covered the worktops and stuck to the floor.

Then I took a good look at Grandma. She was a disaster too.

Her face was striped—blue and white. Flour and blueberry stains filled the creases of her wrinkled cheeks. She had flour streaked across her nose and chin.

"Did you sleep well?" She smiled, and her blue eyes crinkled. With the back of her hand, she wiped a wisp of grey hair from her eyes. Now a glob of blueberry batter nested in the thin strands of her hair.

"I did," Grandpa answered, as a loud shriek rang out from the swamp. "Always do. It's so quiet and peaceful here."

I had to smile. Maybe Grandpa is lucky that he's hard-of-hearing, I thought.

Grandpa headed out the door, and Clark and I brushed ourselves off. Then we took our seats at the table.

In the middle of the table sat another plate of blueberry pancakes. This plate was even bigger than the one Grandma had been holding. And it was stacked high with blueberry pancakes.

"Grandma must think we eat like pigs," Clark leaned over and whispered. "There's enough here for fifty people."

"I know," I groaned. "And we'll have to eat them all. Otherwise, she'll be insulted."

"We do?" Clark gulped.

That's one of the things I really like about my

stepbrother. He believes almost everything I tell him.

"Help yourself," Grandma chirped, carrying two more plates of pancakes to the table. "Don't be shy."

Why did Grandma make all these pancakes? I wondered. *There's no way we could eat all of them. No way.*

I placed a few pancakes on my plate. Grandma heaped about ten on to Clark's plate. His face turned green.

Grandma sat down with us. But her plate remained empty. She didn't take a single pancake.

All those pancakes and she didn't even take one. I don't get it, I thought. *I just don't get it.*

"What's that you're reading, dear?" She pointed to Clark's rolled-up comic, sticking out of the back pocket of his jeans.

"*Creatures from the Muck*," he answered between bites.

"Oh, how interesting," Grandma replied. "I love to read. So does Grandpa Eddie. We read all the time. We love mysteries. 'There's nothing like a good mystery,' Grandpa Eddie always says."

I jumped up from the table. I'd just re-membered—Grandma and Grandpa's presents were still packed in my suitcase.

Books! Mysteries! Dad had told us they loved them.

"Be right back!" I excused myself and dashed upstairs.

I started down the long, winding hall to my room. Then stopped when I heard footsteps.

Who could it be?

I gazed down the dark hall. I gasped when I spotted a shadow moving against the wall.

Someone else was up here.

Someone was creeping towards me.

I pressed my back against the wall. Held my breath and listened.

The shadow slid out of view.

The footsteps grew softer.

Still holding my breath, I inched down the dark twisting hallway. I peeked around a corner. And saw it.

The shadow. Nearly shapeless in the dim light.

It moved slowly along the dark green walls, growing smaller as the footsteps faded in the distance.

I crept swiftly but silently, chasing the shadow through the corridor.

Whose shadow is it? I wondered. Who else is up here?

I crept closer.

The shadow on the wall loomed large again.

My heartbeat quickened as I chased the mysterious shape.

The shadow turned another corner. I hurried to the turn as quietly as I could. And stopped.

Whoever it was—stood right there. Just beyond the turn.

I took a deep breath—and peeked around the corner.

And saw Grandpa Eddie.

Grandpa Eddie—carrying a huge platter stacked high with blueberry pancakes.

How did Grandpa get up here? I wondered. I thought I'd seen him go outside.

Grandpa had come in through another door, I decided. That has to be it. This house is huge. It probably has lots of doors and halls and stairways I haven't discovered yet.

But what was he doing up here carrying an enormous tray of pancakes? Where was he taking them?

What a mystery!

Grandpa Eddie carefully balanced the big silver tray between his hands as he made his way down the hall.

I have to follow him, I thought. I have to see where he's going.

I padded down the hallway. I wasn't too worried about being quiet now. After all, Grandpa didn't hear too well.

I walked only a few metres behind him.

When I heard the sounds, I froze.

Sniffing. Behind me. Furious sniffing.

Oh, no! Charley!

Charley bounded down the hall towards me. Sniffing. Sniffing furiously. Then the dog spotted me—and stopped.

"Good dog," I whispered, trying to shoo him away. "Go back. Go back."

But he broke into a run. Barking his head off.

I grabbed for his collar as he tried to dodge me—to race down the hall to Grandpa.

I grasped the collar tightly. He barked even louder.

"Rose?" Grandpa Eddie called out. "Is that you, Rose?"

"Come on, Charley," I whispered. "Let's get out of here."

I dragged Charley around the corner—before Grandpa could catch me spying on him. Tugging the dog, I ducked into my room.

I sat down on the scratchy blanket for a second to catch my breath. Then I quickly rummaged through my suitcase for Grandma and Grandpa's mystery books.

Where was Grandpa going with those pancakes? I wondered as I hurried down the stairs with the presents.

Why was he creeping along so silently?

It was a mystery I had to solve.

If only I had minded my own business . . .

"Why don't you two go out and play while I clean up these dishes?" Grandma suggested after breakfast. "Then you can help me make my sweet-as-sugar rhubarb pie!"

"Play?" Clark grumbled. "Does she think we're two years old?"

"Let's go out, Clark." I pulled him through the back door. Hanging out in a swamp wasn't exactly my idea of fun. But anything was better than sitting around that creepy old house.

We stepped into the bright sunlight—and I gasped. The hot, steamy air felt like a heavy weight against my skin. I tried to breathe deeply—to shake the smothered feeling I had.

"So what are we going to do?" Clark grumbled, also drawing in a deep breath.

I glanced around and spotted a path. It started at the back of the house and trailed into the swamp.

"Let's explore a little," I suggested.

"I am *not* walking through a swamp," Clark declared. "No way."

"What are you afraid of? Comic-book monsters?" I teased him. "Creatures from the muck?" I laughed.

"You're a riot," Clark muttered, scowling.

We walked a few steps. The sun filtered through the treetops, casting leafy shadows along the trail.

"Snakes," Clark admitted. "I'm afraid of snakes."

"Don't worry," I told him. "I'll watch out for snakes. You watch out for gators."

"Gators?" Clark's eyes opened wide.

"Yeah, sure," I replied. "Swamps are filled with man-eating alligators."

A voice interrupted us. "Gretchen. Clark. Don't stray too far."

I turned and saw Grandpa. He stood a few metres behind us.

What was that in his hand?

A huge saw. Its sharp teeth glinted in the sunlight.

Grandpa headed towards a small, unfinished shed. It stood a little way off the side of the path, tucked between two tall cypress trees.

"Okay!" I shouted to Grandpa. "We won't go far."

"Want to help finish the shed?" he yelled,

waving the saw. "Building things builds confidence, I always say!"

"Um, maybe later," I answered.

"Want to help?" Grandpa shouted again.

Clark cupped his hands around his mouth and yelled, "LA-TER!" Then he turned back towards the path.

And tripped.

Over the dark form that rose up quickly, silently from the muddy grass.

"Gator! Gator!" Clark shrieked.

Grandpa waved his saw wildly. "Later? Later? Okay!"

"Help me! Help me! It's got me!" Clark wailed.

I peered down.

Down at the dark shape in the grass.

And laughed.

"Cypress knee," I said calmly.

Clark turned, his mouth still open in fright. He stared at the knobby form in the grass.

"It's a cypress limb, poking up from the grass," I explained. "It's called a cypress knee. I showed you one yesterday. Remember?"

"I remembered!" he lied. "I just wanted to scare you."

I started to crack a joke, but I saw Clark's whole body trembling as he picked himself up. I felt quite sorry for him. "Let's go back to the house," I suggested. "Grandma is probably waiting for us. To make her sweet-as-sugar rhu-barb pie."

On the way back, I told Clark about seeing Grandpa upstairs, and the huge tray of pancakes he was carrying. But Clark didn't think it was all that strange.

"He probably likes to eat in bed," he said. "Mum and Dad always like breakfast in bed."

"Yeah, maybe," I agreed. But I wasn't convinced. I wasn't convinced at all.

"Well, you two look as if you've had fun!" Grandma chirped when we walked through the door.

Clark and I glanced at each other and shrugged.

"Are you ready to bake?" Grandma smiled. "Everything is ready." She waved at the work-top, at the pie ingredients all lined up.

"Who wants to roll out the dough," she asked, staring straight at me, "while I slice the rhubarb?"

"I suppose I will," I replied.

Clark sighed. "Uh, maybe I'll go into the living room and read my comic," he told Grandma, trying to escape. "Mum says I just get in the way when she cooks."

"Nonsense!" Grandma replied. "You measure out the sugar. Lots and lots of sugar."

I rolled out the pie dough. It seemed like an awful lot of dough. But then—what did I know?

I'm never around when Mum bakes. She says I get in the way too.

When the dough had been rolled flat, Grandma took over. "Okay, children. You sit down at the table and have a nice glass of milk. I'll finish up."

Clark and I weren't thirsty. But we didn't feel like arguing. We drank our milk and watched Grandma finish making the pie.

No—not one pie. *Three* pies.

"Grandma, how come you're making *three* pies?" I asked.

"I always like to have a little extra," she explained. "Just in case company drops in."

Company? I thought. Company?

I stared at Grandma.

Is she totally mad?

Who did she think was coming to visit? She lives in the middle of nowhere!

What is going on around here? I wondered.

Is Grandma really expecting visitors?

Why does she make so much extra food?

"Work builds thirst!"Grandpa announced, banging open the kitchen door. He headed for the refrigerator. "See! I'm right!" Grandpa pointed to our empty milk glasses. "Are you two ready to help with the shed now?"

"Eddie, the children didn't come here to work!" Grandma scolded. "Why don't you two have some fun exploring the house? There are endless rooms. I'm sure you'll find some wonderful treasures."

"Great idea!" Grandpa's face lit up with a smile. But it faded quickly. "Just one warning. You'll find a locked room. At the end of the hall on the second floor. Now pay attention, children. Stay away from that room."

"Why? What's in it?" Clark demanded.

Grandma and Grandpa exchanged worried glances. Grandma's face turned bright pink.

"It's a supply room," Grandpa replied. "We've stored away things in there. Old things. Fragile

47

things. Things that could easily break. So just stay away."

Clark and I took off. We were glad to get away. Grandma Rose and Grandpa Eddie were nice—but weird.

The kitchen, living room, and dining room took up most of the ground floor. And we'd seen them already.

There was a library on the ground floor too. But the books in there were old and dusty. They made me sneeze. Nothing very exciting in there. So Clark and I went upstairs. To the first floor.

We made our way past our bedrooms.

Past the little hall window.

We followed the twists and turns of the dim hallway—until we came to the next room.

Grandma and Grandpa's bedroom.

"I don't think we should go in there," I told Clark. "I don't think Grandma and Grandpa want us snooping through their things."

"Come on!" he urged. "Don't you want to check it out? For pancake crumbs." He laughed.

I shoved Clark hard.

"Hey!" he grumbled. His glasses slid down his nose. "It was just a joke."

I left my stepbrother in the hall and opened the door to the next room. The door was made of heavy, dark wood. It groaned when I pushed it.

I fumbled in the dark for the light switch.

The room glowed a sickly yellow—from a single, dirty bulb, dangling from the ceiling.

In the dreary light, I could make out cartons. A room full of cartons. Stacks and stacks of them.

"Hey! Maybe there's some cool stuff in these boxes," Clark said, pushing past me.

Clark began to pry one open. "Whatever is in here must be pretty big," he said, pointing to the carton's bulging sides.

I peered over Clark's shoulder. The room smelled so musty and sour. I held my nose and squinted in the dim light. Waiting for Clark to reveal what was inside the box.

Clark struggled with the cardboard flaps—and finally they sprang open.

"I don't believe this!" he exclaimed.

"What?" I demanded, craning my neck. "What?"

"Newspapers. Old newspapers," Clark reported.

We lifted the top layers of newspapers to reveal—more newspapers. Old, yellowed newspapers.

We opened five more boxes.

Newspapers.

All the cartons were stuffed with newspapers. A room filled with cartons and cartons of newspapers. Dating way back to before Dad was born. More than fifty years of newspapers.

49

Why would anyone want to save all this stuff? I wondered.

"Whoa!" Clark leaned over a box across the room. "You're not going to believe what's in this one!"

"What? What's in it?"

"Magazines." Clark grinned.

My brother was starting to get on my nerves. But I made my way across the room. I liked magazines. Old ones and new ones.

I shoved my hand deep inside the magazine box and lifted out a stack.

I felt something tickle the palm of my hand. Under the magazines.

I peeked underneath.

And screamed.

Hundreds of cockroaches skittered through my fingers.

I flung the magazines to the floor.

I shook my hand hard, trying to shake the ugly brown insects off. "Help me!" I wailed. "Get them off me!"

I felt prickly legs scurrying up my arm.

I struggled to brush them off—but there were dozens of them!

Clark grabbed a magazine from the floor and tried to swat them off. But as he whacked my arm, *more* roaches flew out from the pages.

On to my T-shirt. My neck. My face!

"Ow! Nooo!" I shrieked. "Help me! Help me!"

I felt a cockroach skitter across my chin.

I brushed it off—and slapped one off my cheek.

Frantic, I grabbed Clark's comic from his back pocket—and began batting at the scurrying cockroaches. Brushing and batting. Brushing and batting.

"Gretchen! Stop!" I heard Clark scream. "Stop! They're all off. Stop!"

Gasping for breath, I peered down.

He was right. They were gone.

But my body still itched. I wondered if I would itch for ever.

I went out into the hall and sat on the floor. I had to wait for my heart to stop pounding before I could speak. "That was so gross," I finally moaned. "Totally gross."

"Tell me about it." Clark sighed. "Did you have to use my comic?" He held it up by a corner. Not sure if it was safe to stuff back in his pocket.

My skin still felt as if prickly roach legs were crawling all over it. I shuddered—and brushed myself off one last time.

"Okay." I stood up and peered down the dreary hallway. "Let's see what's in the next room."

"Really?" Clark asked. "You really want to?"

"Why not?" I told him. "I'm not afraid of little insects. Are you?"

Clark hated insects. I knew he did. Big ones *and* little ones. But he wouldn't admit it. So he led the way into the next room.

We pushed open the heavy door—and peered inside.

"Wow! Look at all this junk!" My stepbrother stood in the middle of the room. Spinning round and round. Taking it all in.

A room filled with toys and games. Really old toys and games. Mountains of them.

In one corner stood a rusty tricycle. The big front tyre was missing.

"I bet this belonged to Dad," I said. It was hard to imagine Dad as a little kid, riding this trike.

I honked the horn. It still worked.

Clark pulled out a dusty chess set from a banged-up wooden box. He began setting up the board while I hunted through the rest of the junk.

I found a teddy bear with its head badly twisted out of shape.

A box that held a single roller skate.

A stuffed toy monkey with one of its arms yanked off.

I rummaged through bags and bags of little toy soldiers, their uniforms faded, their faces rubbed off.

Then I spotted an antique toy chest. It had a golden carousel painted on it, dulled with age.

I lifted the dusty lid. A porcelain doll rested face down inside the chest.

I lifted her gently. And turned her face towards me.

Fine cracks ran across her delicate cheeks. A small chip marred the tip of her nose.

Then I stared into her eyes—and gasped.

She had no eyes.

No eyes at all.

Just two black holes cut out of the space below her small forehead. Two gaping black holes.

"*These* are Grandma's treasures?" I croaked. "It's all junk!"

I dropped the doll into the chest.

And heard a squeak.

From the other side of the room. Next to the door.

I turned and saw a rocking horse, rocking back and forth.

"Clark, did you push that horse?" I demanded.

"No," Clark replied, softly, watching the horse rock back and forth. Back and forth. Squeaking.

"Let's get out of here," I said. "This room is starting to give me the creeps."

"Me, too," Clark said. "Someone beheaded the

queen in the chess set. Chewed her head right off."

Clark leaped over some boxes and jumped into the hall.

I turned for one last look before I clicked off the light. *Totally creepy*.

"Clark?"

Where did he go?

I glanced up and down the long hall.

No sign of him. But he was there just a second ago. Standing in the doorway.

"Clark? Where are you?"

I walked down the corridor, following its twists and turns.

A queasy feeling settled in my stomach. My heart began to race.

"Clark? This isn't funny."

No answer.

"Clark? Where *are* you?"

"BOOOOOO!"

I let out a long shrill scream.

Clark stepped out from behind me, bent over with laughter. "Gotcha!" he cried. "Gotcha big-time!"

"That wasn't funny, Clark," I growled at him. "It was just stupid. I wasn't even scared."

He rolled his eyes. "Why can't you just admit it, Gretchen? Admit it—just once. You were totally scared."

"*Not!*" I insisted. "You just surprised me. That's all." I stuffed my hands in my jeans pockets so Clark wouldn't see them shaking. "You're a real jerk," I told him.

"Well, Grandma told us to have fun. And *that* was fun!" he teased. "So where should we go now?"

"*We* aren't going anywhere," I told him angrily. "I'm going to hide in my room and read."

"Hey! Great idea!" Clark exclaimed. "Let's play hide-and-seek!"

"*Play?* Did I hear you say *play*?" I asked sarcastically. "I thought you said that only two-year-olds *play*."

"This is different," Clark explained. "Hide-and-seek in this house is definitely not for babies."

"Clark, I am not—"

He didn't let me finish. "NOT IT!" he cried. Then he took off, running down the hall to hide.

"I don't want to be It," I grumbled. "I don't want to play hide-and-seek."

Okay, I told myself. Get this over with. Find Clark fast. Then you can go to your room and read.

I started to count by fives.

"Five, ten, fifteen, twenty . . ." I called out, counting to one hundred. Then I started down the dark hall. When I reached the end, the hall turned—revealing an old winding staircase that led up to the second floor.

I started to climb the dusty, wooden stairs. They wound round and round. I looked up ahead, but I couldn't see where the steps led.

I couldn't even see my own feet. It was totally black in there.

The stairs creaked and groaned with every step I took. A thick layer of grime coated the banister—but I held on to it anyway. And I groped my way up—up the dark, winding staircase.

Breathing hard, I climbed higher and higher. The dust in the air stuck in my throat. It smelled sour and old.

I finally reached the top of the staircase and peered down the second-floor hallway. It looked like the one below—with the same twists and turns.

The same dark green walls. The same dim shaft of light that entered from a single window.

I slowly moved down the hall and opened the first door I reached.

It was a huge room. Almost as big as the living room. But totally empty.

The next room was just as large. Just as empty.

I moved carefully down the dark hall.

It was really hot up here. Beads of sweat dripped down the sides of my face. I blotted them with the sleeve of my T-shirt.

The next room I entered was small. Well, not exactly small, but the smallest I'd seen so far. Against one wall stood an old player piano.

If it wasn't so gross up here, I'd come back to this room, I thought. I'd come back and see if the old piano worked.

But right now all I wanted to do was find Clark in his hiding place. And leave.

I walked a little farther.

Rounded a corner.

And choked on a scream—as I started to fall.

No floor!

No floor at all beneath my feet!

My hand shot out in the dark, fumbling for something to grab on to.

I grabbed something hard—an old banister.

And held on. Held on. Held on.

I gripped it tightly with both hands and swung myself back. Back up to the solid hallway floor.

My heart pounding, I stared down into the gaping black hole where I had fallen. A hole where an old staircase once stood. Now rotted away with age.

I let out a long sigh. "I'll get you for this, Clark," I cried out loud. "I told you I didn't want to play."

I hurried down the hall, searching for my stepbrother. Searching quickly. To get this stupid game over with.

And then I stopped.

And stared—at the door at the end of the hall.

A door with a shiny metal lock.

I moved slowly towards the door. A tarnished silver key rested in the keyhole.

What is inside there? I wondered. Why is it locked?

I stepped closer.

Why don't Grandma and Grandpa want us in that room?

They said it was a supply room.

Practically every room in this weird old house is a storage room, I thought. Why don't they want us to open *that* door?

I stood in front of the door.

I reached out my hand.

And wrapped my fingers around the silver key.

No.

I pulled my hand away from the doorknob.

I have to find Clark, I decided. I'm tired of playing this stupid game. I'm tired of being It.

Then I had a great idea.

I'll hide! I'll trick Clark into being It!

I'll hide and Clark will get bored waiting for me to find him. He'll have to look for me!

Perfect! I thought. Now . . . where shall I hide?

I searched the rest of the rooms on the second floor—scouting out a good hiding place. But the rooms up here were all empty. Nothing to slip behind.

Nothing to crawl under.

I returned to the little room with the player piano. Maybe I can figure out a way to hide behind that, I thought.

I tried to push the piano away from the wall.

Just enough so I could squeeze behind it. But it was far too heavy. I couldn't budge it.

I made my way back to the door with the silver key—the locked room.

I peered up and down the dim hall. Had I searched everywhere? Had I missed a room?

That's when I spotted it.

A small door. A door in the wall.

A door I hadn't noticed before.

A door to a dumb waiter.

I'd seen dumb waiters in films. In big, old houses like this one. They were little lifts that carried food and dishes from one floor to another. Pretty cool.

A dumb waiter! I thought. A perfect place to hide! I turned and started towards it—when I heard a crash. A crash—like the sound of a plate dropping.

A crash coming from the other side of the door with the silver key.

I pressed my ear against the door. I heard footsteps.

So *that's* where Clark is hiding! I realized. He is such a cheat! He hid in the one place he knew I wouldn't look!

He hid in the room Grandma and Grandpa told us to stay out of.

Well, Clark, I thought. Too bad for you. I've found you!

I slipped my fingers around the key and

turned it. The lock sprang open with a sharp click. I yanked open the door.

And stared at a hideous monster.

I nearly fell into the room.

I couldn't move. Couldn't back away. Couldn't take my eyes off him.

A living, breathing monster. At least three metres tall.

Standing inside the locked room.

I gaped at his big, furry body. A body like a gorilla—with leaves and tree roots and sand tangled in his fur. His head was scaly, with snapping rows of jagged alligator teeth.

A foul stench filled the room. The putrid smell of decay. The smell of the swamp.

My stomach heaved.

The creature raised his eyes to me—bulging eyes set into the sides of his enormous head.

He held me in his stare for a moment. Then he glanced down at his hairy paws—where he was balancing a tall stack of pancakes.

He began stuffing the pancakes into his

mouth. Devouring them. Gnashing them with his jagged teeth.

Still gripping the door handle, I stared at the monster as he ate. He jammed another stack of pancakes down his throat. He swallowed them whole and grunted with pleasure.

His horrible alligator eyes went wide. The thick veins in his neck throbbed as he ate.

I tried to call for help. To scream. But when I opened my mouth, no sound came out.

With one hand the monster shoved pancakes into his mouth—stacks at a time. With the other, he scratched at one of his furry legs.

Scratched and scratched. Until he found a big black beetle, nesting in his fur.

He held the beetle up to the side of his head— to one of his bulging eyes.

The beetle's legs waved in the air.

He glared at the beetle. At the waving legs.

Then he popped it into his mouth—and chomped down on its shiny black shell with a sickening crunch.

Blueberries and beetle juice oozed from his mouth.

Run! I told myself. *Run!* But I was too terrified to move.

The creature reached down for another stack of pancakes.

I forced myself to take a small step back— into the hall.

The monster jerked his head up.

He glared at me. Then he let out a deep growl.

He let the pancakes slide to the floor and lumbered towards me.

I ran, screaming for help as I charged into the hall.

"Gretchen! Gretchen! What's wrong?" Clark turned the corner at the end of the corridor.

"A monster! In the locked room! Hurry!" I shrieked. "Hurry! Get help!"

I leaped down the stairs. "Grandma! Grandpa!" I cried out. "A monster!"

I turned to see if the beast was following me— and realized that Clark hadn't moved.

"There's a monster in there!" I wailed. "Get away, Clark! Get away!"

He sniggered. "You must think I'm pretty stupid to fall for that one."

Clark headed towards the door of the monster's room. Grinning.

"No! Please!" I pleaded. "I'm telling the truth!"

"You just want to scare me. To get even."

"I'm not kidding, Clark! Don't go in there!" I shrieked. "DON'T!"

Clark reached the door. "Here I am, swamp monster!" he called out as he stepped into the room. "Come and get me!"

A second later Clark's terrified screams echoed from the room.

The creature roared over Clark's cries.

Charley bounded up the stairs, barking wildly.

"Run! Run!" Clark came bursting from the room, waving his arms. "A monster! A swamp monster!"

We tore down the stairs, dragging Charley with us. Charley fought hard. He wanted to turn around and charge back up the steps.

"Charley, come!" I pleaded. "Come!"

But Charley sat down on a step and howled. He wouldn't budge.

A bellow thundered through the hall.

Oh, no! He's coming! He's coming after us!

"PLEASE, CHARLEY!" I begged, yanking on his collar. "PLEASE!"

Clark stood on the steps, frozen in fear.

"Help me, Clark!" I pleaded. "Don't just stand there. Help me!"

The swamp monster pounded down the hall. The old stairway quaked under our feet.

"He's coming to get us," Clark whispered. He still hadn't moved.

I grabbed my stepbrother's T-shirt and yanked him hard. "Help me, Clark!" I screamed. "Push Charley!"

We struggled down the stairs. I tugged Charley and Clark shoved him from behind.

"Grandma! Grandpa!" I cried out.

No answer.

The monster's roar grew louder. Closer.

"Lock Charley in the bathroom!" I ordered Clark when we reached the first floor. "He'll be safe there. I'll find Grandma and Grandpa."

I charged down to the kitchen. "Grandma! Grandpa!" I yelled. "A monster!"

No one in the kitchen.

I flew into the living room. "Where are you? Help!"

Not in the living room.

I searched the library. Empty.

I ran back up the stairs. I checked their bedroom and all the other rooms on the first floor.

I couldn't find them anywhere.

Where are they? Where could they be? I asked myself.

Clark stepped out of the bathroom—just in

time to hear the monster's footsteps rumbling above us.

"W-where's Grandma and Grandpa?" he stammered.

"I—I don't know. I can't find them!"

"Did you check outside?" His voice came out in a squeak.

That's it! I thought. Don't panic, Gretchen. They must be outside. Probably in the back. Grandpa is probably working on the shed.

We bolted down the stairs and into the kitchen.

We stopped at the back door. Stared out across the swamp. To the shed.

No one back there.

"Where are—?" Clark began.

"Listen!" I cut Clark off. "Can you hear that?"

The sound of a car—starting up.

"Grandpa and Grandma's car! It's back! It's fixed!" I shouted.

We followed the sound of the engine. It was coming from the front of the house.

We ran to the front door and peered out the window.

There they were!

"Huh?" I cried out in shock.

My grandparents were backing down the driveway.

They were driving away!

"No—wait! Wait!" I screamed, turning the lock.

"They can't hear you!" Clark shouted. "Open the door! Open it!"

I yanked on the door. I pulled it as hard as I could. I turned the lock again.

"Hurry!" Clark shrieked. "They're leaving us here!"

I tugged and tugged. And turned the knob frantically.

Then I realized the horrible truth.

"It's bolted from the outside!" I told Clark. "They've locked us in!"

"How could they do this to us?" I wailed. "How could they leave us here? Why did they lock us in?"

The ceiling shook above our heads. Shook hard. Hard enough to send the pictures on the living-room wall crashing to the floor.

"What was that?" Clark's eyebrows shot up.

"The monster! He's coming after us!" I croaked. "We have to get out of here! We have to find help!"

Clark and I ran back to the kitchen. To the kitchen door.

I twisted the doorknob. Pulled as hard as I could. But this door was also jammed shut— barred from the outside.

We ran through the house.

We checked all the side doors.

All stuck. All of them—bolted shut from the other side.

The monster's footsteps rumbled above us.

How could Grandma and Grandpa do this to us? How could they? How could they? The question screamed in my head as I charged into the library. To the window.

The only window on the whole ground floor.

Our only escape now.

I struggled to shove the window up.

It wouldn't budge.

I pounded on the wooden sash with my fists.

"Look!" Clark choked. He pointed to the grimy pane. "Look!"

Two rusty nails. Driven into the wooden sash. Nailing the window shut—from the outside.

Nailing us in.

How could they do this to us? How could they? I chanted silently. *How could they?*

"We have to break the glass!" I turned to Clark. "It's the only way out!"

"Okay!" Clark cried. He leaned forward and began beating his fists against the pane.

"Are you nuts?" I screamed at him. "Find something stronger to—"

But the rest of my sentence was lost—lost in a deafening crash from above. Followed by the thundering clatter of piano keys.

"Wh-what's he doing?" Clark stammered.

"There's an old piano up there. It sounds as if he's throwing it across the room!"

The floors, the walls, the library ceiling—everything quaked—as the monster hurled the piano across the second-floor room. Over and over again.

A porcelain vase, a crystal dish, little glass animals flew from a nearby table and shattered at our feet.

I threw my hands over my head as the library books spilled from their shelves.

Clark and I huddled together. On the floor. Waiting for the avalanche of books to end.

Waiting for the monster to stop.

We huddled there until the house grew silent.

A final book tumbled from a shelf. It landed on a small table next to me.

"Hand me that!" I ordered Clark, pointing to a heavy brass candlestick next to the book. "Stand back."

I turned to the window. I pulled back my arm to swing the heavy candlestick—when I heard the whimpering.

Charley's whimpering. From upstairs.

"Oh, no!" I gasped. "The monster—he's got Charley!"

I ran for the stairway, clutching the candlestick in one hand, dragging Clark with the other.

I had to save Charley! I had to!

I raced up the stairs. I stopped when I reached the top.

My heart pounded in my chest as I peered down the hall.

The corridor was empty.

I crept towards the bathroom. Except for Clark's raspy breathing and the thudding of my heart, the house was still.

As I neared the bathroom, the bathroom door came into view.

Shut.

I gripped the doorknob. It slipped in my sweat-drenched hand.

I opened the door a crack and peeked inside. But I couldn't see anything.

I could feel Clark breathing down my neck as I pushed the door open a bit more.

A bit more.

"Charley!" I cried out with relief.

Charley sat in the bathtub. Curled up in a corner. Scared—but safe.

He gazed up at us with his big brown eyes. He wagged his tail weakly. Then he began to bark.

"Shhhh!" I whispered, petting him. "Please, Charley. Don't let the monster hear you. Quiet, boy."

Charley barked even louder.

So loud that we almost didn't hear the car pull up outside.

"Shhhh!" I urged Charley. I turned to Clark. "Did you hear that?"

His mouth dropped open. "A car door!"

"Yes!" I cried.

"Grandma and Grandpa are back!" Clark shouted. "I'll bet they've brought help!"

"Stay," I commanded Charley as we eased out of the bathroom. "Good boy. Stay."

Clark slammed the door behind us, and we bolted down the stairs.

"I knew they'd be back! I knew they wouldn't just leave us!" I flew down the steps, two at a time.

And heard the engine start.

Heard the car rumble away.

Heard the tyres crunch down the driveway.

"Noooo!" I shouted as I reached the front door. "Don't go! Don't go!"

I pounded the door with my fists. I kicked it hard. And then I saw the pink slip of paper on the floor, slipped under the door.

A message. I picked it up with a trembling hand. And started to read:

We're not coming back. Until next week. Sorry, kids. But work is taking much longer than we thought.

A phone message—from Mum and Dad.

Grandma and Grandpa hadn't come back, I realized. Mr Donner, from the general store, had driven over to deliver this phone message.

The roar of the monster tore through my thoughts.

I spun around.

Clark was gone.

"Clark!" I shouted. "Where are you?"

The monster's growls grew louder. Meaner.

"Clark!" I called out again. "Clark!"

"Gretchen—come quickly!" I heard his desperate cry from the kitchen.

76

"Gretchen! Gretchen!"

As I charged through the living room, he shouted my name over and over again. Each time his voice grew higher, more excited.

"I'm coming!" I yelled. "Hold on, Clark. I'm coming!"

I rounded the couch—and tripped over a footstool. My head hit the floor hard.

Clark continued to cry out my name, but his voice seemed distant now. So far away.

My head throbbed with pain.

I struggled to stand, and the room spun around me.

"Gre-tchen! Gre-tchen!"

He sounded more frantic than ever.

"I'm coming!" I said through a dizzy haze.

Then I heard the monster's bellow. It thundered through the house.

I have to get to Clark. He's in trouble! The monster has him! I realized.

I stumbled through the living room. Towards the kitchen.

The creature's roars shook the walls.

"Hold on, Clark!" I tried to shout, but my voice came out in a moan. "I'm coming!"

I stumbled into the kitchen.

"Gretchen!" Clark stood next to the refrigerator.

Alone.

"Where is he?" I cried. My eyes darted around the room, searching for the monster.

"Wh-where's who?" Clark stammered.

"The monster!" I yelled.

"Upstairs," Clark replied, puzzled. "What took you so long to get here?"

Clark didn't wait for an answer. "Look at this." He pointed to the refrigerator. I turned and saw two letters stuck there with magnets.

"You were screaming like a *maniac* to show me that?" I shrieked. "I nearly killed myself! I thought the monster had grabbed you!"

Clark's hand trembled as he lifted the envelopes from the refrigerator. "It's two letters addressed to us. From Grandma and Grandpa."

I stared at the envelopes in Clark's hand. They were addressed to us, just as he said. And they were numbered, one and two.

"They left us letters?" I couldn't believe it.

Clark ripped open the first envelope. The

paper shook in his hands as he began to read it to himself.

His eyes scanned the paper. He mumbled as he read. I couldn't understand what he was saying.

"Let me have that!" I reached out for the letter, but Clark jerked back. He held the paper tightly and continued to read.

"Clark, what does it say?" I demanded.

He ignored me. He pushed his glasses up on his nose and kept on reading. Mumbling.

I watched Clark as he read.

I watched his eyes move down the page.

I watched his eyes grow wide with horror.

"Clark!" I shouted impatiently. "What does it say?"

Clark began to read the letter out loud. "'Dear Gretchen and Clark,'" he started. The paper fluttered between his trembling fingers.

"'We're sorry to do this to you, but we had to leave. A few weeks ago, a swamp monster invaded our house. We captured it in the room upstairs. Then we didn't know what to do with it. We didn't have a car, so we couldn't get to a phone to call for help.

"'We've lived in terror for the past few weeks. We were afraid to let the monster out. It's so loud and angry all the time. We know it would have killed us.'"

My knees started to wobble as Clark continued.

"'We didn't want to tell your parents about the creature. If we did, they wouldn't have let you come. We don't get many visitors here. We wanted so much to see you. But I guess we were wrong. You should have gone to Atlanta with your mother and father. I guess we were wrong to let you stay.'"

"They guess they were wrong! *They guess!*" I shrieked. "Can you *believe* them?"

Clark peered up from the letter. His face was white. Even his freckles seemed to disappear. He shook his head, stunned.

Then he continued to read our grandparents' letter. "'We've been feeding the creature, slipping food through an opening Grandpa sawed in the bottom of the door. The monster eats a lot. But we had to feed him. We were afraid not to.

"'We know it's unfair to run off now. But we're just going for help. We'll be back—as soon as we can find someone. Someone who knows what to do with this horrible beast.

"'Sorry, kids. We really are—but we had to bolt you inside the house. To make sure you didn't wander into the swamp by yourselves. It's not safe out there.'"

Were they for *real*?

"Not safe *out there!*" I cried. "They left us in this house with a killer monster—and they say it's not safe *out there*! They're both crazy, Clark. Totally crazy!"

Clark nodded and continued reading. "'Sorry, kids. We really, really are sorry. But just remember one thing: You are perfectly safe as long as . . .'"

The monster upstairs let out a loud bellow. And Clark dropped the letter.

I watched in horror as it sailed through the air.

Floated down to the floor.

And slid under the refrigerator.

"Get it, Clark!" I yelled. "Quick!"

Clark stretched out on the floor and shoved his fingers under the refrigerator. But his fingers only managed to brush the tip of the paper, shoving it back.

"Stop!" I yelled. "You're pushing it away!"

But Clark didn't listen.

He shoved his hand in deeper. Groping for the paper.

Pushing it back. Farther and farther.

Until we couldn't see it any more.

"What did it say?" I hollered. "You read the letter! We're perfectly safe as long as . . . what?"

"I—I didn't get to that part," Clark stammered.

I wanted to strangle him.

I spun around. And frantically searched for something to slip under the refrigerator—to ease out the letter.

But I couldn't find anything slim enough or long enough. Everything was far too big to fit underneath.

Clark tore open the kitchen cabinets and drawers looking for something we could use.

The monster stomped on the floor above us.

The ceiling quaked.

A dish fell off the worktop and shattered on the cold grey tiles. Shattered into a thousand tiny pieces.

"Oh, no," I moaned, staring up at the ceiling, watching the paint crack and crumble. "He's down to the first floor. He's coming closer."

"We're doomed," Clark groaned. "He's going to catch us and—"

"Clark. We have to move the refrigerator. We have to find out what it says in the rest of that letter!"

Clark and I tugged on the refrigerator. We pushed and tugged with all our strength.

Upstairs, the monster roared an angry roar.

We tugged harder.

The refrigerator began to move.

Clark knelt down and peered underneath it. "Push!" he told me. "Push! I can see a corner of the letter! Push—just a little more!"

I gave the refrigerator one more hard shove— and Clark had it! He grasped the corner of the letter between his thumb and index finger. And pulled it out.

He shook the paper, to free a clump of dust that clung to it.

"Just read it!" I shouted at him. "Read it!"

Clark started to read again. "'You are perfectly safe as long as . . .'"

I held my breath, waiting for Clark to finish the sentence. Waiting to find out how we could keep ourselves safe.

"'You are perfectly safe'," Clark read, "'as long as you do not open the door and let the monster out.'"

"That's it?" My jaw dropped. "It's too late for that! It's too late! Did they say anything else? They must have said something else!"

"There's a little more." Clark read on:

"'Please. Please stay away from that room. Do not open that door.'"

"Too late!" I wailed. "It's too late!"

"'If the monster escapes, you will have no choice. You will have to find a way to kill it.'" Clark looked up from the letter. "That's it, Gretchen. That's all it says. *You will have to find a way to kill it.*"

"Quick!" I ordered Clark. "Open the other letter. It'll probably tell us more. It has to!"

Clark started to tear open the second envelope when we heard the heavy footsteps.

Footsteps downstairs.

In the next room—the living room.

"Hurry, Clark! Open it!"

Clark's fingers fumbled as he tried to rip through the sealed envelope. But he stopped when we heard the creature's breathing.

Deep, wheezing breaths.

Coming nearer.

My heart thumped wildly as the monster's wheezing grew louder.

"He—he's coming for us!" Clark cried, stuffing the unopened envelope in his pocket.

"The dining room!" I shouted. "Head for the dining room!"

"What are we going to do? How can we kill it?" Clark cried as we bolted from the kitchen.

"We—*owwww!*" A sharp pain shot up my leg as I ran smack into the dining-room table.

I clutched my knee. I tried to bend it. But the pain tore through it.

I spun around.

And there he stood.

The swamp monster.

In the kitchen—lumbering towards us hungrily.

The monster glared at me with his horrible bulging eyes. I watched the veins in his head throb as he let out a long, low growl.

I stared at those huge, pulsing veins. Stared as they beat against his coarse alligator skin.

"Run, Gretchen!" Clark pulled me from behind. He yanked me out of the dining room. We dived towards the stairs.

"We need a place to hide," Clark panted as we fled to the first floor. "We have to hide until Grandma and Grandpa come back with help."

"They're not coming back!" I screamed at him. "They're not coming back with help!"

"They said they would," Clark insisted. "They said so in the letter."

"Clark, you are such a jerk." We reached the top of the stairs. I stopped to catch my breath. "Who is going to believe them?" I said, gulping air. "Who's going to believe they have a swamp monster trapped in their house?"

Clark didn't reply.

I answered for him. "No one! That's who. Everyone they tell the story to will think they're nuts."

"Someone might believe them." Clark's voice cracked. "Someone might want to help."

"Yeah, right. *'Will you help us kill a swamp monster?'* they'll ask. I bet they'll get loads of volunteers!" I rolled my eyes.

I stopped yelling at Clark when I heard the monster's heavy breathing. I spun around—and saw the creature.

He stood at the bottom of the stairs. Eyeing us. Drooling hungrily.

Clark and I backed slowly away from the top of the stairs.

The monster followed us with his eyes.

"We have to kill it," Clark whispered. "That's what the letter said. We have to kill it. But how?"

"I have an idea!" I told Clark. "Follow me!"

We turned and ran. As we charged past the bathroom, we heard Charley whimpering.

"Let's get Charley!" Clark stopped running. "It's too dangerous to leave him closed up in there. We have to take him with us."

"We can't, Clark," I replied. "He'll be okay. Don't worry."

I wasn't as sure about that as I sounded. But there was no time to stop for Charley now—

because the monster had reached the first floor.

There he stood. Looming at the end of the hall.

He raised his hands up over his head. I saw that he held the wooden footstool I had tripped over in the living room.

His eyes burned with anger.

He glared at me, then growled a loud, savage growl. A stream of thick white drool dribbled down his chin.

He licked the drool away with a reptile tongue—and smashed the stool down across his leg. It splintered into two jagged pieces.

He raised the pieces and hurled them at us.

"Let's go!" Clark shrieked as the footstool bounced off the wall.

We ran up the stairs. Up to the second floor.

The monster lumbered after us. The whole house shook with each heavy step he took.

"He's coming!" Clark cried. "What are we going to do? You said you had an idea. What?"

"There's a collapsed stairway up here," I told Clark, running as fast as I could through the dark, twisting hall. "It's totally fallen down. Just a big hole. When we turn the corner, grab on to the railing. The monster will chase us around the corner—and he'll fall down the open stairway."

The roar of the monster thundered in my ears. I saw him plodding down the hall after us.

"Come on, Clark! Hurry!"

"What if it doesn't work?" Clark demanded, very frightened. "What if the fall only *hurts* him? Won't it make him even more angry?"

"Don't ask questions, Clark," I replied impatiently. "It's got to work! It's got to!"

We started to run again.

The monster howled. Howled with rage.

"There's the turn, Clark. Up ahead."

The creature roared. Only steps behind us.

My heart pounded hard. My chest felt as if it were about to explode. "Grab the railing, Clark. Or else you'll drop to the bottom. Here goes!"

We turned the corner.

We both threw our hands up. And grabbed the railing.

Our bodies slammed hard against the wall— then dangled over the black, empty hole.

The creature turned the corner.

Would my plan work? Would he fall to his death?

Was this the way to kill a monster?

The beast whirled around the corner.

Staggered on the edge of the hole.

His head jerked to face us. His eyes glowed red.

He opened his mouth in an ugly growl. He swayed, trying to keep his balance. Then he plunged down the open staircase.

I heard him land with a heavy thud.

Clark and I hung on to the rotted banister. It creaked under the strain of our weight.

My hands ached. My fingers were numb. I knew I couldn't hold on much longer.

We listened.

Silence.

The creature didn't move.

I looked down, but it was too dark to see.

"My fingers are slipping," Clark groaned. Then he swung out his foot, searching with his trainer for the hallway floor.

Hand over hand, he inched his way along the

banister to the safety of the hall. I followed.

We peered down into the black hole once more. But it was so black down there—we couldn't make out a thing. Dark and silent. Totally silent.

"We did it! We're safe!" I cheered. "We killed the monster!"

Clark and I jumped up and down in celebration. "We did it! We did it!"

We ran downstairs. We let Charley out of the bathroom.

"Everything is okay, Charley." I hugged my dog. "We did it, boy," I told him. "We killed the swamp monster."

"Let's get out of here," Clark urged. "We can walk to town. Call Mum and Dad from the general store. Tell them to pick us up—now!"

We were so happy, we practically danced down the steps. The three of us headed into the library. "Stand back," I told Clark. "And hold Charley. I'll break the window, and we'll get out of here."

I glanced around the room, searching for the heavy brass candlestick to break the glass. It wasn't there.

"Wait here," I told Clark. "I left the candlestick up in the bathroom. I'll be right back."

I sprinted out of the library.

I couldn't wait to break out of this creepy place. To leave this horrible swamp. And tell

Mum and Dad how stupid they were to dump us here in a house with a real, live monster inside.

I ran through the living room—to the stairs.

I jogged up three steps—and stopped.

Stopped when I heard the low groan.

It can't be, I thought. Maybe it's Charley. Maybe Charley is growling.

I listened.

And heard it again.

Not a dog growl. Definitely not a dog growl.

Then I heard the rumbling footsteps, the footsteps of the swamp monster, coming from somewhere nearby.

Closer.

Closer.

"Clark!" I staggered back into the library. My legs were shaking. My whole body trembled. "He's not dead!" I cried. "The monster isn't dead!"

The library was empty.

"Clark? Where are you?" I shouted.

"In the kitchen," he called. "Feeding Charley."

I raced into the kitchen. Clark and Charley sat on the floor. Charley was lapping up a bowl of water.

"The fall didn't kill him! The monster isn't dead!" I shrieked.

Clark gasped in horror. "He must be really angry now. He must be furious. What are we going to do?"

My eyes darted around the kitchen. "Put Charley in there," I ordered. "In that cupboard. I have another idea."

"I hope it's better than your last idea," Clark moaned.

"Do *you* have an idea?" I yelled at him. "Do you?"

He didn't.

Clark dragged Charley across the kitchen. "Gretchen, this isn't a cupboard. It's some kind of room."

"I don't care what it is," I hollered. "Just put Charley in there."

On the worktop sat one of Grandma's rhubarb pies. "The monster hasn't eaten since this morning," I told Clark. "We'll put this pie out on the worktop where he'll see it."

"But that will only slow him down for a second," Clark whined. He shut Charley in the room. "He'll gobble the pie in one bite. Then he'll come after us again."

"No, he won't," I insisted. "We're going to *poison* the pie. We'll put stuff in it. Enough stuff to kill him!"

"I don't know, Gretchen," Clark argued. "I don't think that's going to work."

Charley whimpered behind the closed door—as if he agreed.

"We have no choice!" I snapped. "We have to try *something*!"

I found a fork and carefully lifted up the pie crust with it.

Then I searched the cabinet under the kitchen sink. It was filthy under there. Damp, with green mould growing on the pipes.

I found a jar of turpentine sitting on a shelf right at the front. The lid was screwed on tight. I had to twist it hard to open it.

I slowly poured the entire jar of turpentine into the pie.

"Yuck! That stuff stinks," Clark said, holding his nose.

I studied the pie. It was wet and runny now. "I think we need something to soak up the turpentine," I told Clark. "This should do it!" I held up a can of drain cleaner.

I sprinkled the blue drain-cleaner crystals over the pie. They made the rhubarb bubble and fizz.

Clark leaped back. "I think that's enough," he said.

I ignored him.

I stuck my head under the sink and came up with two jars. "Rat poison!" I exclaimed, reading the dirty label on one of them. "Excellent." The other jar was filled with ammonia.

"Hurry!" Clark urged. "I can hear the monster. He's coming."

I sprinkled the pie with the rat poison and poured in the ammonia too.

The monster's groans came closer. Each time he groaned or growled, I jumped.

I found an old can of orange paint and dumped it into the pie.

"That's enough! We have enough!" Clark insisted in a panic.

"Okay. Okay. I just want to make sure this works."

I shoved in a handful of mothballs.

"Hurry!" Clark urged. "Close it up. He's coming!"

The monster's footsteps pounded the living-room floor.

"Hurry!" Clark begged.

I sprayed the top of the pie with insect repellent.

"Gretchen!" Clark pleaded with me.

I placed the poisoned pie on the worktop.

It's so sweet, your teeth will fall out after one bite. Grandma's words came back to me.

It'd better do more than that! I told myself. It'd better kill a monster!

"Here he comes!" Clark cried.

We ducked under the kitchen table.

The monster stomped into the kitchen. Peering out from under the table, I could see him swing his arms wildly. He knocked over dishes, pots, glasses. Everything in sight.

Then my heart stopped when I saw the big creature turn.

He hesitated. Then he took a step towards the kitchen table. Another step. Another.

Clark and I huddled together under the table. We were both trembling so hard, the table shook.

The swamp monster can see us under here! I
realized.

We're trapped.

What is he going to do?

Clark and I held on to each other. The monster stepped up to the table—so close I could smell the sour odour of his thick fur.

Clark started to let out soft, whimpering sounds.

I clapped my hands over his mouth. I shut my eyes.

Please go away, I prayed. Please, monster, don't *see* us.

I heard the creature sniffing. Like a dog trying to sniff out a bone.

When I opened my eyes, he had moved away from the table.

"Whew!" I breathed a long, silent sigh of relief.

The monster rumbled around the room.

Sniffing loudly, urgently.

He sniffed the refrigerator.

He lumbered over to the stove and sniffed some more. He plodded around the room. Sniffing.

He can smell us. He can smell Clark and me, I thought. *Please, see the pie. See the pie.*

The creature stomped back to the stove.

Sniffing.

He bent down and peered into the oven. Then he ripped the oven door off its hinges and hurled it across the room.

The door hit the wall with a loud crash. Clark jumped in fright and banged his head on the table. He let out a low moan.

I moaned too. "Look," I whispered.

The creature was eating—but he wasn't eating *our* pie. There were two pies still in the oven. And the creature was stuffing himself with them.

Oh, no, I thought. He'll eat those pies. Then he'll be full. He won't eat *our* pie! We're as good as dead.

The monster hungrily jammed the two pies into his mouth. He practically swallowed them whole. Then he lumbered to the centre of the room.

Sniffing.

Yes! He's still hungry! I thought. *Eat our pie. Eat our pie*, I chanted to myself.

I peered out from under the table—and saw the creature, heading towards the worktop. *Yes!*

He stopped.

And sniffed.

He saw the pie.

100

He eyed it for a moment. Then he lifted it to his mouth and shoved it in.

Yes! I cheered silently. *He's eating it! He's eating our pie!*

He chomped away at the pie. Chomped and shoved more into his huge mouth. Chomped and shoved. Chomped and shoved.

He licked his big lips as he ate.

He licked his paws.

He rubbed his stomach.

"Oh, no!" I groaned. "He *likes* it!"

I watched the monster shove the last bit of pie into his mouth.

Then he flicked his reptile tongue in and out, licking up every last crumb from the pie tin.

"It isn't working," I moaned to Clark. "He loves it."

"Now what are we going to do?" he whispered back. He hugged his knees tightly to his chest to keep them from shaking.

The monster let out a long groan.

I peered out from under the table. I saw the creature's eyes bug out. They practically popped out of his head!

A gurgling, choking sound escaped his throat.

He grasped his neck with his two hairy paws.

He groaned again.

His stomach rumbled—a deep rumble. He clutched his stomach and doubled over.

He uttered a weak cry of pain—and surprise.

Then he dropped dead on the kitchen floor.

"We did it! We did it!" I cheered. "We killed the swamp monster!"

I pulled Clark out from under the table.

I studied the creature from across the room. I was sure he was dead—but I still didn't want to get too close.

The monster's scaly eyelids were closed.

I stared at his chest—to see if it moved. To see if he was breathing.

His chest remained still.

I stared at him a few moments longer.

He didn't stir.

Clark peered over my shoulder. "Is—is he really dead?" he stammered.

"Yes!" I was sure of it now. Totally sure. "We did it!" I cried. I jumped up and down joyfully. "We killed the monster! We killed him!"

Clark reached into his back pocket—for his comic book, *Creatures from the Muck*. He hurled it across the room. It hit the monster in the head and fell to the floor.

"I never want to read about swamp monsters again. Never!" Clark cried. "Let's get out of here!"

Charley scratched at the door. When we opened it, he leaped out and jumped all over us. "It's okay, boy," I told him, trying to calm him down. "It's okay."

I peered into the room where we had locked

Charley. "Hey, Clark, I think there's a door in here," I said. "A door that leads out!"

I stepped into the small, dark space—and stumbled over a broom lying on the floor.

I squinted in the darkness.

Two rusty shovels leaned against the wall to my right. On the left sat a coil of old hose.

In front of me I saw the door. A door with a large glass window.

I looked out the window—out to the backyard. To the path that ran through the swamp.

Does that path lead through the swamp to town? I wondered. I decided it was worth a try.

"We're almost out of here!" I declared. "We're almost free!"

I turned the doorknob, but the door was locked. Bolted from the other side, like all the doors in the house.

"It's jammed shut," I told Clark. "But I'll break the window and we'll climb out. No problem."

The shovels against the wall were big and heavy. I gripped the handle of one with both hands and took aim.

I swung it back—and felt the floor quake.

I spun around—and heard the roar.

The roar of the swamp monster.

He wasn't dead.

The creature rumbled into the doorway.

Clark and I both shrieked as he took a giant step into the room. His hideous head made a scraping sound as it brushed against the frame of the door. But he didn't even seem to notice.

Clark and I pressed against the wall.

Charley backed into a corner, whimpering. Frightened.

We were trapped.

No way out.

Nowhere to run.

The monster's eyes shifted from Charley, to me, to Clark. They rested on Clark for a moment. Then the creature lifted his head and wailed.

"He—he's going to get me first," Clark cried. "I—I shouldn't have thrown the comic at him. I shouldn't have hit him on the head."

"He's going to get *us*, you jerk!" I shouted at him. "Because *we* tried to *kill* him!"

That shut Clark up.

I have to do something, I thought. *I have to do something*. But what? *What?*

The swamp monster staggered forward.

He opened his snout with a snap—and bared jagged yellow teeth.

Sharp yellow teeth, dripping with saliva.

His eyes glowed red as he moved forward. Clomping closer and closer.

I glanced down and realized that I was still holding the shovel. I lifted it with two hands—and thrust it forward. Jabbing—jabbing at the air between the creature and me.

"Back!" I screamed. "Get back! Leave us alone!"

The monster grunted.

"Get back! Get back!" I swung the shovel wildly. "Go away!"

I swung at the creature.

I swung—and hit his stomach with a sickening *thwack*.

The room went silent.

Then the monster tossed back his head and let out a piercing howl.

He stumbled forward. Swiped the shovel from my hand. And tossed it out the door. Tossed it as if it were a toothpick.

I gasped as it crashed to the kitchen floor.

I eyed the other shovel leaning against the wall. The monster followed my gaze.

He snatched it up and broke it in half with his bare hands. Then he threw the pieces into the kitchen.

What can I do? I have to do something!

And then it came to me!

The letter.

The second letter from Grandma and Grandpa—the one we hadn't opened yet!

"Clark! Quick! The second letter," I cried. "Maybe it will tell us what to do! Read it!"

Clark stared at me. Frozen. His eyes on the raging monster.

"Clark!" I said, through clenched teeth. "Open . . . the . . . letter. NOW!"

He reached into his jeans pocket with a trembling hand. He fumbled with the flap.

"Hurry, Clark!" I pleaded.

He finally managed to tear a hole in the corner of the envelope.

And then I screamed.

The monster dived forward.

He grabbed my arm. He yanked it hard.

And pulled me towards him.

The monster pulled me close.

I stared up into his hideous face—and gasped.

His eyes were deep, dark pools—with tiny worms swimming in them!

I twisted my head away—so I wouldn't have to stare into those horrible, wormy eyes.

The creature gripped me tighter.

His hot, sour breath swept over my cheeks.

He opened his jaws wide.

His mouth was filled with insects! I saw them crawling up and down his tongue.

I screamed. And struggled against the monster's hold. But he clutched me too tightly.

"Let me go!" I shrieked. "Please—!"

The monster bellowed in reply, hitting me with a blast of his hot breath.

He smells like a swamp, I realized as I fought against his grasp. *He is a swamp. He's like a living swamp.*

With my free hand, I pounded on the

creature's arm. I nearly gagged when I felt the moss. His whole body was covered with a layer of wet moss!

"Let me go!" I pleaded. "Please—let me go!"

Clark leaped forward. He grabbed my arm and tried to tug me away. "Leave her alone!" he shrieked.

Charley charged out of his corner. His lip curled back and he let out a low snarl. Then he sank his teeth into the monster's hairy leg.

Startled, the monster jerked away, dragging me along with him.

But Charley wouldn't give up. I glanced down to see him dig his teeth deep into the monster's foot.

With a growl, the beast raised his foot. And with one fierce shake, he hurled Charley across the room.

"Charley!" I cried out. "Charley!"

I heard Charley whimper on the other side of the room.

"He's okay," Clark said, breathlessly. He tugged harder on my arm, trying to wrestle me free.

With another angry growl, the beast swung at Clark. Shoved him hard against the wall. Then the monster leaned down—and pulled me up to his face.

He opened his mouth.

His disgusting, insect-infested tongue rolled out.

And he LICKED me.

He ran his hot, bumpy tongue up and down my arm.

Then he lowered his enormous teeth—as he prepared to chew off my hand.

"Nooooo!" A horrified shriek tore from my throat.

The monster's jaw swung down. His mouth gaped open. The insects swarmed over his yellow teeth. He lowered his mouth to my hand.

Then he stopped.

And let me go.

He backed away, staring at me. Staring at my arm, eyes bulging.

I stared at my arm too. It was covered with disgusting, monster saliva.

The monster raised his hands and clutched at his throat now. Choking. Choking on something.

He raised his wet eyes to me.

"You—you human?" he choked out.

"He can *talk*!" Clark gasped.

"You human? You human?" he demanded.

"Y-yes, I'm a human," I stammered.

The monster threw back his head and groaned. "Oh, no. I'm *allergic* to humans."

His eyes rolled up.

He staggered forward and collapsed against the door to the outside. It crashed open under his heavy weight. Moonlight streamed in.

He lay there on his stomach. He didn't move.

I rubbed my wet arm and stared down at the swamp monster.

Was he really dead this time?

"Gretchen! Let's go!" Clark yanked me towards the open door.

We stepped over the monster. I glanced down at the creature one last time.

His eyes were shut. He didn't breathe. He didn't move.

"Come *on*, Gretchen!" Clark pleaded.

Is he really dead? I stared at the swamp monster. I wasn't totally sure. But I did know one thing—I wasn't going to hang around to find out.

Clark and I ran out through the broken door. We found Charley already there, waiting for us. We bolted down the path—away from the house. Into the swamp.

I was so surprised to find it was dark out. Had we really fought the swamp monster all day?

A pale moon hung over the cypress trees, casting an eerie glow over them.

The mud rose up over my ankles as we made

our way through the marshy ground. Through the tall weeds. Through a blanket of heavy mist.

My shoes plunged into deep pools of water.

Tripped over upraised roots.

I swiped at the long beards of grey that hung from the trees. Swiped them from my face as we headed deeper and deeper into the swamp.

When the house was no longer in view, we stopped running. Stopped to catch our breath.

I listened in the darkness for footsteps.

The swamp monster's footsteps.

There weren't any.

"We did it! We killed the monster!" My voice rang out in the night.

"And we escaped!" Clark cheered. "We're free! We're okay!"

"Yes!" I shouted. "We really did it!"

Now that we had stopped running for our lives, we stepped through the swamp carefully. Leaping over the inky puddles and gnarled tree roots.

The night air echoed with strange sounds.

Low gurgling. Scampering footsteps. Piercing cries.

But I didn't care.

I had already battled my worst nightmare— the swamp monster. Battled him and won.

"Hey! Clark!" I suddenly remembered the other letter! "We didn't read Grandma and Grandpa's letter. The second letter!"

"So what?" Clark replied. "We don't have to read it. The monster is dead. We killed it. Just as they told us to do in the first letter."

"Where is it? Where's the letter?" I demanded. "Take it out, Clark." I stopped walking. "I want to know what it says."

Clark pulled the crumpled envelope from his jeans pocket. As he smoothed out the wrinkles, a fierce animal cry cut through the swamp.

"I—I don't think we should stop now," Clark said. "We can read it later. After we reach town. After we call Mum and Dad."

"Read it now," I insisted. "Come on. Don't you want to know what it says?"

"No," Clark declared.

"Well, I do," I told him.

"Okay. Okay." Clark ripped open the envelope and slipped out the letter.

A light wind began to blow, carrying the sharp animal cries to us.

The dark trees rustled over our heads.

Clark began to read slowly, struggling to see in the dim moonlight. "'Dear Gretchen and Clark. We hope you children are safe and well. We forgot one word of warning in the first letter.

"'If the monster gets out . . . and you do kill it . . . and escape from the house—stay on the road. Do NOT go into the swamp.'"

Clark rolled his eyes. He let out a loud groan.

"Keep reading!" I shouted. "Read!"

He squinted in the dark and went on. "'The monster's brothers and sisters live in the swamp—dozens of them. We think they are out there. Waiting for him.'"

My heart started to race as Clark continued. "'We've seen the monsters in the swamp. We've heard them whistling to each other every night. They're unhappy their brother was captured. They're waiting for him to return. So whatever you do, stay out of the swamp. It's not safe out there. Stay out of the swamp! Good luck! We love you.'"

Clark's hands dropped to his sides. The letter fell to the marshy ground.

I turned slowly, staring out at the shifting shadows.

"Gretchen." Clark choked out my name. "Can you hear that? What is that sound? What is it?"

"Uh . . . it sounds like a whistle."

"Th-that's what I thought," he whispered. "What do we do now? Any ideas?"

"No, Clark," I replied softly. "I don't have any more ideas. How about you?"

Goosebumps

Legend of the
Lost Legend

Justin Clarke tugged his gloves under the sleeves of his heavy blue parka. Then he shielded his eyes with one hand and searched all around. "I can't see Dad," he told his sister, Marissa. "Can you?"

"I can't see *anything*!" Marissa cried, shouting over the wind. "All I can see is *ice*!"

The sledge dogs barked and shook themselves, eager to start moving again.

Justin narrowed his eyes, squinting to the right, then the left. The ice stretched smooth and shiny, silvery under the bright sunlight.

In the distance, it darkened to blue. Darker. Darker. Until the blue ice appeared to melt into the sky. Justin couldn't see where the ice ended and the sky began.

"It's cold," Marissa murmured. A sharp gust of wind blew the parka hood off her red hair. She instantly reached up with both hands and pulled it back in place.

Justin rubbed his stub of a nose. He pressed his furry gloves against his frozen cheeks, trying to warm them.

The dogs tugged. Justin grabbed the handle of the dog-sledge to keep it from sliding away.

"What do we do now?" Marissa asked. Justin could hear a slight tremble in her voice. He knew his sister was as frightened as he was.

He stepped on to the sledge runner. "Keep going, I guess. Keep going until we find Dad."

Marissa shook her head. She held her hood in place with both hands. "Maybe we should stay right here," she suggested. "If we stay here, it will be easier for Dad to find *us*."

Justin stared hard at her. Why does Marissa look so different? he wondered. Then he realized—the cold had made her freckles disappear!

"It's too cold to stay in one place," he said. "It will be warmer if we keep moving."

He helped her on to the back of the sledge. At twelve, he was only a year older than Marissa. But he was big and athletic, and she was tiny and skinny.

The dogs grunted and impatiently pawed the silvery ice.

"I *hate* Antarctica!" Marissa wailed, grabbing the sledge handle with both hands. "I hate everything about it. I can't even *spell* it!"

Uh-oh, thought Justin. Here she goes. Once

Marissa started complaining, she never stopped.

"We'll be okay," he said quickly. "As soon as we find Dad, everything will be okay. And we'll have some amazing adventures."

"I *hate* amazing adventures!" Marissa declared. "Almost as much as I hate Antarctica! I can't believe he brought us to this awful place—and then lost us!"

Justin gazed up at the sky. The sun had started to set. Wide streaks of golden light sparkled over the ice.

"We'll find Dad really soon," he told Marissa. "I know we will." He lowered the hood over his forehead. "Let's get going, okay? Before we freeze." He snapped the line and, in a deep voice, called out to the six dogs, *"Mush! Mush!"*

The dogs lowered their heads and moved forwards with a burst of speed. The sledge jerked hard as it started to slide.

"Whoooooaaa!"

Justin let out a startled shriek as he felt himself start to fall.

His gloved hands flew off the sledge handle. He frantically groped for it.

Missed.

And fell off the sledge. He fell hard on to his back on the ice.

"Ooooof!" He felt the breath whoosh from his lungs.

His arms and legs kicked the air, like a bug on its back.

He struggled to a sitting position. Blinking. The ice shimmering all around him. Shimmering so brightly, he could barely see the sledge as it sped away.

"Justin—I can't stop it!" Marissa's shrill shriek sounded tiny against the steady rush of cold wind.

"Marissa—!" He tried to call to her.

"I can't stop it! Help me! Help!" Her cry already so far away.

Justin leapt to his feet and started to run after the sledge.

He fell again. Face first this time.

How can I run in snowshoes? he wondered. They're like wearing tennis rackets on my feet!

He had no choice. He jumped back up and started to run.

He had to catch the sledge. He couldn't let Marissa face the cold and the endless ice on her own.

"I'm coming!" he shouted. "Marissa—I'm coming!"

He lowered his head against the onrushing wind. He dug the snowshoes into the snowy surface of the ice. One step. Then another. Then another.

Running hard, he raised his head and squinted into the distance. The sledge was a dark blur against the glowing ice. A *tiny* blur.

"Marissa—!" he gasped. "Stop the sledge! Pull the line! Pull it!"

But he knew she couldn't hear him.

His heart thudded in his chest. He felt a sharp stab of pain in his side. His legs ached from lifting the heavy snowshoes.

But he kept moving. He didn't slow down.

When he gazed up again, the sledge appeared larger. Closer.

"Huh?" His cry sent a puff of white steam floating above his head.

Am I catching up? he asked himself.

Yes!

The sledge appeared clearer now. Closer.

He could see Marissa, holding on with one hand, waving frantically to him with the other.

"How—how did you stop the sledge?" he choked out as he staggered up to her.

Her blue eyes were wide with fear. Her chin trembled. "I didn't stop it," she told him.

"But—"

"It stopped itself," Marissa explained. "The dogs—they all stopped. I'm frightened, Justin. They stopped all by themselves." She pointed. "Look at them."

Justin turned to the dogs at the front of the sledge. All six of them had their heads lowered, their backs arched. They all whimpered and shook, huddled together.

"Something is frightening them," Justin murmured. He felt a sudden chill of fear.

"They won't move," Marissa said. "They just

hunch together, whimpering. What are we going to do?"

Justin didn't reply. He stared past the sledge. Past the frightened dogs.

He stared at an amazing sight.

A blue lake. Almost perfectly round, as if someone had carved it out of the ice. A pool of water reflecting the clear blue of the sky.

"Oh, wow!" Marissa gasped. She saw it too.

In the centre of the small lake, they both saw a creature sitting on a large chunk of ice. It had its head lowered, staring back at them.

A sea lion.

A blue sea lion!

"It's the one Dad is looking for!" Justin cried. He stepped up beside his sister. They both stared in amazement at the magical creature.

"The only blue sea lion in the world," Marissa murmured. "A creature from a myth. No one even believes it is real."

Where is Dad? Justin wondered, not taking his eyes from the enormous blue animal. How can Dad be missing this?

He brought us all the way to Antarctica to search for this creature. And now he's lost— lost!—and Marissa and I are the only ones to see it.

"Do you think we can get closer to it?" Marissa asked. "Can we walk up to the edge of the water and see it better?"

125

Justin hesitated. "Dad said it has strange powers," he told his sister. "Maybe we should stay back here."

"But I want to see it better," she protested.

She started to step off the sledge—then stopped.

They both heard the rumbling sound at the same time.

A deep rumble, low at first and then louder.

"Where is it coming from?" Marissa asked in a whisper, her eyes suddenly wide with fear.

"The sea lion?" Justin guessed. "Did it roar?"

No.

They heard it again. Louder this time. Like thunder.

Thunder . . . *beneath* them.

And this time the ground shook.

Justin heard a cracking sound. He looked down in time to see the ice start to break.

"Ohh!" A frightened cry escaped his throat. He grabbed for the back of the sledge and pulled himself on to it.

"What is happening?" Marissa cried. She grasped the sledge handle with both hands.

Another rumble of thunder beneath them.

The sledge tilted and started to rock.

The sound of cracking ice drowned out the low rumble.

Ice cracked all around. The ground appeared to split open.

The blue sea lion, perched in the centre of the small, round lake, stared back calmly at them.

A loud *crack* made the dogs howl.

The sledge bobbed and tilted. Justin grasped the handle as tightly as he could.

He peered down. And saw that the ground holding them had broken away, broken free.

As the ice cracked, the lake opened up. Water rushed all around.

It's not a lake, Justin realized. It's a hidden *ocean*—under the ice!

"We—we're floating away!" Marissa shrieked.

The dogs howled, drowning out the sound of the cracking ice. Water rushed up over the sides of the sledge. A strong current carried the sledge away.

Justin and Marissa held on tightly, struggling to stay on the rocking, tilting sledge.

The blue sea lion faded into the distance.

And they floated away, bobbing and swaying. Floating out to sea.

"What happens next, Dad?" I asked.

"Yeah. Don't stop there," Marissa begged. "You can't leave Justin and me on a chunk of ice, floating out into the ocean. Go on with the story."

I pulled the top of the sleeping bag up to my chin. Outside our tent, the fire flickered low. I could hear the chittering of insects all around us in the forest.

I peered out through the open tent flap. Too dark to see the trees. I could see a narrow patch of purple sky. No moon. No stars at all.

Is anything darker than a forest? I wondered.

We had a paraffin lamp inside the tent. It sent warm yellow light around us. But no heat.

Dad buttoned the top button of his sweater. It had been hot in the tent when we came in after dinner. But now a damp chill had fallen over us.

"That's all for tonight," Dad said, scratching his brown beard.

"But what happens next?" Marissa demanded. "Go on with the story, Dad. Please!"

"Yeah," I agreed. "Do we float out to sea? How do we get back? Do you show up and rescue Marissa and me?"

Dad shrugged his big shoulders. Under the woolly sweater, he looked like a big, brown bear. "I don't know," he replied. "I don't know what happens next."

He sighed and bent over his sleeping bag. He has a big stomach, and it's hard for him to bend over. He started to unfold the sleeping bag.

"I haven't thought of an ending to the story yet," Dad said softly. "Maybe I'll dream a good ending tonight."

Marissa and I both groaned. We hate it when Dad stops a story in the middle. He always leaves us in terrible danger. And sometimes we have to wait for days to find out if we survive.

Dad sat down on the tent floor. He groaned as he pulled off his boots. Then he struggled to squeeze into the sleeping bag.

"Good night," Marissa said, yawning. "I'm so tired."

I felt tired too. We'd trudged through the forest since early morning, cutting our own path through the trees, and rocks, and tangled weeds.

"Justin, do me a favour," Dad said. He pointed

to the paraffin lamp. "Turn that off, okay?"

"No problem," I said.

I leaned forward. Reached for the lamp.

My hand bumped it. Knocked it on its side.

And in seconds, the tent was ablaze with orange and yellow flames.

I let out a sick cry and struggled to pull myself out of the sleeping bag.

Dad climbed to his feet first. I'd never seen him move so fast.

He picked up a section of the canvas tent floor and smothered the flames on the tent wall.

"Dad—sorry!" I managed to choke out. I finally struggled out of the sleeping bag.

Luckily, the flames had only caught on one wall. I have too good an imagination. I'd instantly pictured us surrounded by fire.

I think I get my imagination from Dad. Sometimes it comes in handy. Sometimes it doesn't.

Now I was breathing hard, my whole body trembling. "Sorry," I repeated.

"That was close!" Marissa cried, shivering. "Justin is such a klutz!" She had scrambled to the tent flap, ready to run outside.

Dad shook his head. "It only burned a small

131

hole," he reported. "Here. I can cover it with this." He spread the section of canvas floor over the hole.

"This thing burns pretty fast," I murmured.

Dad grunted but didn't reply.

"I'd hate to be in the middle of the forest without a tent," Marissa declared. "Especially in *this* weird country."

"Everything is fine," Dad said softly, still fiddling with the tent wall. "But no thanks to either of you," he added sourly.

"Huh? What do you mean?" I demanded, straightening a leg of my pyjamas.

"You haven't been much help," Dad complained.

"What did *I* do?" Marissa asked shrilly. "I didn't try to burn the tent down."

"You wandered off and got lost this morning," Dad reminded her.

"I thought I saw a weird animal," Marissa replied.

"It was probably a squirrel," I chimed in. "Or her shadow."

"Give me a break, Justin," Marissa muttered.

"Then tonight you both refused to get firewood," Dad accused.

"We were tired," I explained.

"And we didn't know where to look," Marissa added.

"In a forest?" Dad cried. "You don't know

where to look for firewood *in a forest*? How about on the *ground*?"

Dad was getting steamed up.

Maybe he's right, I thought. Maybe Marissa and I should try to be a little more helpful.

After all, this was a very important trip for Dad. And it was really great of him to bring us along.

My dad is Richard Clarke. Maybe you've heard of him. He's a very famous writer, storyteller and story collector.

Dad travels all over the world, searching for stories. All kinds of stories. Then he puts them in books. He has published ten books of stories. And he goes all over the country, telling some of the stories he has hunted down.

He has been on a lot of exciting trips. But this one was special. He brought Marissa and me to Europe—to this forest in the tiny country of Brovania—because of a very special search.

Dad had kept the whole thing as a surprise. But he told us about it as we made our way through the forest that morning.

"We've come to Brovania to search for the Lost Legend," he explained. He pulled a large black beetle from his beard and tossed it away.

"The Lost Legend is a very old manuscript. It is said to be hidden away in a silver chest," Dad continued as we walked. "It hasn't been seen for five hundred years."

"Wow," Marissa murmured from far behind us. She kept stopping to look at insects and wild flowers. Dad and I had to keep waiting for her to catch up.

"What is the legend about?" I asked.

Dad shifted the heavy equipment pack on his back. "No one knows what the legend is about," he replied. "Because it has been lost for so long."

He used his machete to hack away a tall clump of weeds. Then we followed him through a narrow opening in the trees.

The trees were so thick and leafy overhead, little sunlight could get through. Even though it was still morning, the forest stretched as dark as night.

"If we find the Lost Legend, we'll be very lucky," Dad said. "It will change our lives."

"What do you mean?" I asked.

His expression turned solemn. "The ancient manuscript of the Lost Legend is worth a fortune," he replied. "The whole world is curious about it. The whole world wants to read it. Because no one knows who wrote it—or what it's about."

I thought about it all day as we twisted our way through the forest. What if *I'm* the one to find it? I asked myself.

What if I look down and see the silver chest? Hidden between two rocks, maybe. Or half-buried in the dirt with only part of its silver lid poking up.

Wouldn't that be cool? Wouldn't that be *awesome*?

I pictured how happy Dad would be. And I thought about how rich and famous I would be too. I'd be a hero. A real hero.

That's what I thought about all day.

But so far, I knew I hadn't been much of a hero. In fact, I'd nearly burned down the tent.

And Dad was already grumbling that Marissa and I hadn't been much help.

I'll be more helpful, I promised silently that night. I snuggled lower into the sleeping bag, trying to get warm.

On the other side of the tent, I could hear Dad snoring lightly. Dad can fall asleep in seconds. And he's such a sound sleeper, you practically have to hit him on the head to wake him up!

Marissa and I are not like Dad. It takes us *hours* to fall asleep. And the tiniest, tiniest sound wakes us up instantly.

So now I lay on my back in the sleeping bag, staring up at the dark ceiling of the tent. Trying to clear my mind. Trying not to think about anything.

Trying to fall asleep . . . asleep . . . asleep.

I had almost drifted off—when an animal howl cut through the silence.

An angry howl. A menacing howl.

So close!

Right outside the tent.

I jerked straight up. Wide awake. Breathing hard.

I knew this wasn't a story-book creature.

This creature was real.

The air in the tent felt cold against my hot skin. I realized that I was sweating.

I listened hard.

And heard a shuffling sound. A low growl. The crackle of heavy paws over the leafy forest ground.

My heart pounding, I slid the sleeping bag down. Started to crawl out of it.

"Oh!" I let out a whispered cry as someone pushed past me.

"Dad—?"

No. I could still hear Dad's steady snores from across the tent.

I knew it would take more than a terrifying animal howl to wake Dad up!

"Marissa—" I whispered.

"Sssshh." She held a finger up to her mouth as she crawled towards the tent flap. "I heard it too."

I moved quickly beside her. We stopped in front of the closed flap.

"It's some kind of animal," Marissa whispered.

"Maybe it's a *werewolf*!" I whispered back.

There goes my wild imagination again.

But aren't werewolves supposed to live deep in the forests of Europe? I think that's where all the old werewolf movies took place. In a forest just like this one.

I heard another low growl.

I grabbed the tent flap and pulled it up. Cold air rushed in. A gust of wind ruffled my pyjama top.

I peered out into the night. A mist had fallen over the small clearing where we had set up the tent. Pale moonlight shining through the mist turned everything a shade of blue.

"What *is* it?" Marissa whispered from close behind me. "Can you see it?"

I couldn't see any animal. Only swirls of blue mist.

"Get back inside," Marissa ordered.

I heard more shuffling sounds. A loud sniff.

"Hurry. Get back in," Marissa urged.

"Just wait," I whispered. I had to see what was out there. I had to see what was making those noises.

I shivered. The air felt heavy and damp.

Wisps of the blue fog seemed to cling to me.

I took a step out of the tent. The ground sent a shock of cold up from my bare feet.

I held my breath and took another step.

And saw the creature.

A dog. A big dog, tall. Like a shepherd, only with long, white fur. The white fur shimmered like silver under the misty moonlight. The dog had his head lowered. He sniffed the ground.

As I stared at the animal, he raised his head and turned to me. And started to wag his tail.

I love dogs.

I've always loved dogs.

Without thinking, I reached out my arms. And I ran to pet him.

"No! *Don't!*" Marissa screamed.

Too late.

I knelt down and petted the fur on the big dog's back. It felt soft and thick. My hand touched leaves and small twigs tangled in the fur.

The dog's tail wagged furiously. I petted his head. He raised his eyes to me.

"Hey—!" I cried out. The dog had one brown eye, one blue.

"He might be a wolf!" Marissa called. I turned to see that she had taken only one step from the tent. She clung to the flap, ready to duck inside at any instant.

"He's not a wolf. He's a dog," I told her. I studied him again. "At least, I don't *think* he's a wolf," I added. "I mean, he's too friendly to be a wolf."

I rubbed the top of his head. Then I scratched the thick, white fur on his chest. I pulled blades of dried grass and weeds from his fur.

The dog wagged his tail happily.

"What is he doing out here?" Marissa demanded in a loud whisper. "Is he a wild dog? Justin—he might be dangerous."

The dog licked my hand.

"I don't think he's too dangerous," I told her.

"But maybe he's part of a pack," Marissa warned. She let go of the tent flap and took another step across the ground towards me. "Maybe the other wild dogs sent him out as a scout. Maybe there are a *hundred* of them!"

I climbed to my feet and glanced around. Squinting through the blue mist, I could see the tall, dark trees that circled the clearing. A half-moon floated low over the trees, shimmery through the fog.

I listened hard.

Silence.

"I think this guy is alone," I told my sister.

Marissa gazed down at the dog. "Remember that story Dad used to tell about the ghost dog?" she asked. "Remember? The dog used to appear outside someone's house. It was such a cute little dog. Very sweet and cuddly. It would tilt its head up towards the moon and let out an '*eeeh eeeh*' sound, as if it were laughing.

"The dog was so cute, people had to come out and pet it. And when they did, the dog would start to bark. It would call its ghost dog friends.

"The friends were mean and ugly. And they

would circle the person, circle faster and faster. And then gobble the poor victim up. And the last thing the victim would see was the cute, cuddly dog tilting back its head, laughing '*eeeh eeeh*', laughing at the moon.

"Remember that story?" Marissa demanded.

"No, I don't," I told her. "I don't think that's one of Dad's stories. It isn't good enough. I think it's one of yours."

Marissa thinks she's a great storyteller like Dad. But her stories are pretty dumb.

Whoever heard of a laughing dog?

She took another step towards the dog and me. I shivered. The forest air was cold and damp, too cold to be out in pyjamas and bare feet.

"If he's a wild dog, he could be dangerous," Marissa repeated.

"He seems gentle enough," I said. I petted his head again. And as my hand slid down the fur on the back of the dog's neck, I felt something hard.

At first I thought it was another dead leaf matted in his thick, white fur. I wrapped my hand around it.

Not a leaf. A collar. A leather dog collar.

"It's not a wild dog," I told my sister. "He has a collar. He must belong to someone."

"Maybe he ran away and got lost," Marissa said, kneeling beside the dog. "Maybe his owner is searching the forest for him."

"Maybe," I agreed. I tugged the collar up over the thick fur. The dog turned his head and licked my hand.

"Does it have an ID tag or a licence?" Marissa asked.

"That's what I'm looking for," I replied. "Whoa. Hold on. There is something tucked under the collar."

I pulled out a folded-up wad of paper. Squinting in the dim light, I started to unfold it. "It's a note," I told Marissa.

"Maybe it has the owner's address or a phone number on it," she said.

I finished unfolding it and held the sheet of paper up close to my face to read it.

"Well? What does it say?" Marissa demanded.

I read the handwritten words silently to myself—and gasped in surprise.

"Justin—what does it say?" Marissa repeated.

Marissa tried to grab the note from my hand. But I swung it away from her.

"It's a very short note," I told her. I held it up again and read it out loud:

"'I KNOW WHY YOU'RE HERE. FOLLOW SILVERDOG.'"

"Silverdog?" Marissa lowered her gaze to the dog. "Silverdog?"

His ears perked up.

"He knows his name," I said. I ran my eyes over the paper, trying to see if I had missed anything. But that's all there was. No name at the bottom. Nothing else.

Marissa took the note from me and read it for herself. "'I KNOW WHY YOU'RE HERE'," she repeated.

I shivered. The blue fog lowered around us. "We'd better show this to Dad," I said.

Marissa agreed. We turned and hurried to the tent. I glanced back to make sure the dog wasn't leaving. Silverdog had walked over to a clump of tall weeds and was sniffing around them.

"Hurry," I whispered to Marissa.

We both made our way to Dad's sleeping bag. He was sound asleep on his back, making soft blowing sounds through his lips.

I dropped to my knees and leaned over him. "Dad? Dad?"

He didn't stir.

"Dad? Wake up! It's important! Dad?"

Marissa and I both shouted at him. But he's such a sound sleeper, he didn't hear us.

"Tickle his beard," Marissa suggested. "Sometimes that works."

I tickled his beard.

Nothing. He snored away.

I brought my face down to his ear. "Dad? Dad?"

I tried shaking him by the shoulders. But it was hard to get a good grip under the sleeping bag.

"Dad? Please! Wake up!" Marissa pleaded.

He let out a groan.

"Yes!" I cried. "Dad?"

He rolled on to his side. Sound asleep.

I turned and saw that Marissa had crawled back to the tent opening. She stared out. "The dog is heading towards the trees," she reported. "What should we do?"

"Get dressed," I urged. "Hurry."

We both pulled on the jeans and sweatshirts

we'd been wearing. I got one hiking boot on, then discovered I had a knot in the other shoelace.

By the time I'd pulled the second boot on, Marissa was already back outside. "Where is Silverdog?" I asked, hurrying up beside her.

She pointed through the thickening fog. Clouds had rolled over the moon. The heavy darkness made it almost impossible to see.

But I spotted the big dog loping slowly towards the trees.

"He's leaving!" I gasped. "We have to follow him." I started jogging across the dirt.

Marissa hung back. "Not without Dad," she insisted. "We can't."

"But someone is trying to help us!" I cried. "Someone knows where the Lost Legend is. They sent the dog to bring us."

"It may be a trap," Marissa insisted. "Some kind of evil trick."

"But, Marissa—"

I searched through the fog. Where was the dog? I could barely see him. He had reached the trees on the far side of the clearing.

"Remember the story Dad tells about the forest imp?" Marissa asked. "The imp puts out a trail of flowers and sweets in the forest. And when children follow the trail, it leads them into The Pit With No Bottom. And the kids fall and fall for the rest of their lives. Remember?"

"Marissa—please!" I begged. "No more stories. Silverdog is getting away."

"But—but—" she sputtered. "Dad wouldn't want us to go wandering off on our own in the forest. You *know* he wouldn't. We'll be in real trouble."

"What if we found the Lost Legend?" I replied. "Then what? Then we wouldn't be in trouble— *would* we!"

"No! No way!" Marissa protested, folding her arms over her chest. "We can't go. No way, Justin."

I sighed and shook my head. "I suppose you're right," I said softly. "Let the dog go on its way. Let's get some sleep."

I put my hand on her shoulder and led her back to the tent.

"Are you *crazy*?" Marissa cried. She spun away from me. "We can't let the dog get away! It may lead us right to the Lost Legend!"

She grabbed my hand, gave me a hard tug, and started to run, pulling me across the clearing.

As I ran after her, I tried hard not to let her see the big smile on my face. I *knew* my little trick would work with Marissa. It always does.

If I ever really want to do something, all I have to say is, "Let's not do it."

Marissa always disagrees with me. Always.

That makes it very easy to get her to do what I want.

"Dad said we weren't being helpful," she murmured. "He was giving us a hard time because we wouldn't find firewood. What if we find the Lost Legend? Then we'll be helping him—big-time!"

"Big-time," I repeated.

I pictured Marissa and me handing Dad the silver chest containing the Lost Legend. I pictured the shock on Dad's face. Then I pictured his smile.

Then I pictured the three of us on the TV news programmes. I imagined myself telling everyone how Marissa and I found the valuable old manuscript—without any help from Dad.

My boots clumped over the soft ground. I stopped when we reached the trees.

"There's just one problem," I told Marissa.

She spun around. "What's that?"

"Where's the dog?"

"Huh?" She turned back to the trees.

We both searched the darkness.

The dog had disappeared.

The fog clung to the dark trees. Clouds still covered the moon.

Marissa and I peered into the darkness, listening hard.

I sighed. I felt so disappointed. "I think our adventure is over before it even started," I murmured.

Wrong.

A loud bark made us both jump. "Hey—!" I cried out.

Silverdog barked again. He was calling us!

We stepped between the trees, following the sound.

My boots sank into the soft dirt. Under the tall trees, the sky grew even darker.

"Stick close together," Marissa pleaded. "It's so hard to see."

"We should have brought a torch," I replied. "We left in such a hurry, I didn't think—"

A loud crackling sound made me stop. The crisp thud of paws over dead leaves.

"This way," I urged Marissa. I turned towards the sound. "Silverdog is right up ahead."

I still couldn't see the dog. But I could hear his footsteps over the dry twigs and leaves of the forest floor.

The dog had turned to the left, following a narrow path through the trees. The ground beneath my boots became hard. We both raised our arms in front of our faces as we stepped through a thicket of brambles.

"Ouch!" I cried out as prickly thorns pierced through the sleeve of my sweatshirt.

"Where is that dog taking us?" Marissa asked shrilly. I knew she was trying to sound calm. But I could hear the fear creep into her voice.

"He's taking us to someone who wants to help us," I reminded her. "He's taking us to someone who is going to make us rich and famous.

"Ow!" I pulled a burr from my wrist.

I hoped I was right. I hoped that the note didn't lie. I hoped that the dog was taking us somewhere nice.

The footsteps turned sharply up ahead. I couldn't see a path now. Actually, I couldn't see a metre in front of me!

We kept our arms in front of us, using them as shields. And we pushed our way through a thicket of tall weeds.

"He's speeding up," Marissa whispered.

She was right. I could hear the dog's footsteps moving more rapidly over the ground.

Marissa and I began jogging, eager to keep up. Over our own crunching footsteps, I could hear the dog breathing hard.

The flutter of wings—*many* wings, low overhead—made me duck.

"Were those birds?" Marissa cried. She swallowed hard. And then she added, "Or bats?"

I could still hear the fluttering, in the distance now. The sound sent a chill down my back.

So many flapping wings!

"They were birds," I told Marissa. "They had to be birds."

"Since when do birds fly like that at night?" she demanded.

I didn't answer. Instead, I listened for the dog's footsteps up ahead. They seemed to be slowing down.

We followed the sound through an opening between tall bushes. And stepped into a broad, grassy clearing.

As we made our way into the grass, the clouds floated away from the moon. Under the moonlight, dew-covered grass shimmered like diamonds.

I gazed up from the grass—and gasped in horror.

Marissa grabbed my arm. Her mouth dropped open in shock.

"I don't believe it!" I cried.

I stared at the creature standing a few metres up ahead of us.

Not the dog.

Not Silverdog.

A brown-and-black spotted deer. A stag with antlers that curled up from his head and gleamed in the moonlight.

We had followed the wrong animal.

And now we were hopelessly lost.

The big deer stared at us. Then he turned and trotted across the grass, into the trees on the other side.

Frozen in shock, I watched him disappear. Then I turned to my sister. "We—we made a bad mistake," I managed to choke out. "I thought it was the dog. I really did."

"Let's not panic," Marissa said. She huddled close to me.

A gust of wind made the tall grass whisper and bend. I heard a low moaning sound from the trees behind us. I tried to ignore it.

"You're right. We won't panic," I agreed. But my legs were shaking, and my mouth suddenly felt as dry as cotton.

"We'll go back the way we came," Marissa said. "We didn't walk that far. It shouldn't be too hard to retrace our steps." She glanced around. "Which way did we come?"

I spun around. "That way?" I pointed. "No. That way? No . . ."

I wasn't sure.

"Maybe we should panic," I said.

"Why did we *do* this?" Marissa wailed. "Why were we so stupid?"

"We thought we were helping Dad," I reminded her.

"Now we may never see him again!" she cried.

I wanted to say something to calm her down. But the words caught in my throat.

"This forest goes on for miles and miles!" Marissa continued. "The whole country is probably forest. We'll never find *anyone* who can help us. We—we'll probably be eaten by bears or something before we ever get out."

"Don't say bears," I begged. "There aren't any bears in this forest—are there?"

I shuddered. Dad had told us too many stories that ended with children being eaten by bears. That seemed to be one of Dad's favourite endings.

It was never one of mine.

The wind bent the grass back the other way. In the far distance, I heard the flutter of wings once again.

And over the whisper of the wings, I heard another sound.

A dog bark?

Was I imagining it?

I listened hard. And heard it again. Yes!

I turned and saw the happy expression on Marissa's face. She heard it too. "It's Silverdog!" she cried. "He's calling us!"

"Let's go!" I exclaimed.

I heard another long series of barks. The dog was definitely calling us.

We spun around and ran towards the sound.

Ran back into the trees. Ran through the tall bushes. Leapt over fallen logs. Ran to the barking.

Ran.

Ran full speed.

Until the ground suddenly gave way.

A hole opened up beneath us.

And we started to fall.

"Nooooooo!" I let out a long, terrified wail. "It's The Pit With No Bottom!"

I landed hard on my elbows and knees.

"Ooof!" I let out a groan as my face hit wet dirt.

A bottom.

A very *hard* bottom.

I glanced over at Marissa. She was already climbing to her feet. She brushed dirt and dead leaves off the knees of her jeans.

"What did you yell?" she asked. "I couldn't hear you."

"Uh . . . nothing," I mumbled. "Just yelled."

I glanced up. Marissa and I had tumbled down a short, steep hill. We'd fallen a metre or so.

Not exactly a bottomless pit.

I brushed myself off, hoping Marissa couldn't see how embarrassed I felt.

When we climbed back to the top, Silverdog was waiting for us. The dog raised his head and stared at us with his brown and blue eyes—as if to say, "What is your problem? Why can't you two jerks keep up with me?"

As soon as we joined him at the top of the hill, the big dog turned and loped off, wagging his furry white tail. Every few steps, he glanced back to make sure we were following.

I still felt fairly shaky from the fall. Even though it was such a short drop, I had banged my knees pretty hard. They still ached. My heart still raced.

Dad and his crazy stories, I thought, shaking my head. The Pit With No Bottom . . . why would I even *think* such a crazy thought?

Well . . . what could be crazier than following a big white dog through a Brovanian forest in the middle of the night?

Maybe Marissa and I will have a legend to tell our friends when we're finished, I thought. The Legend of the Two Incredibly Stupid Kids.

Or, maybe we'll find the silver chest containing the Lost Legend—and be rich and famous and make Dad proud.

These were my thoughts as my sister and I followed Silverdog along a curving path through the forest. The dog loped easily between the trees and weeds. And we trotted behind him, eager not to lose him again.

After a few minutes, we stepped into a large patch of tall grass. Marissa and I stopped and watched Silverdog run across the grass, prancing, raising his legs high. He ran to a small cabin on the other side of the grass.

The cabin stood silvery grey under the moonlight. It had one narrow door and one square window under a slanted red roof.

A stone fireplace stood beside the cabin. Some kind of barbecue grill, I guessed. Beside the fireplace, I saw a low pile of firewood, neatly stacked.

I could see no lights on inside the cabin. No sign that anyone lived there.

Silverdog pranced up to the tiny building, pushed the door with his snout, and disappeared inside.

Marissa and I hesitated at the edge of the clearing. We watched the cabin, waiting for someone to come out. The door remained half-open.

We took a few steps closer. "This is where he wanted to bring us," Marissa murmured, her eyes on the cabin door. "Silverdog sure seemed happy to get home. Did you see the way he strutted? Do you think the person who wants to help us is inside?"

"Only one way to find out," I replied.

"The cabin looks almost like a fairy-tale cabin," Marissa said. "Like a cabin in one of Dad's old stories." She laughed, a quiet dry laugh. "Maybe it's made out of cookies and sweets."

"Yeah. Right." I rolled my eyes.

"Do you remember the story—?" she started.

"Please—no stories!" I begged. "Come on. Let's check out the place."

We stepped up to the cabin. The whole building was less than a metre taller than we were!

"Hello?" I called.

No answer.

"Anyone home?" I called, a little louder.

No answer.

I tried one more time. "Hello? Anyone in there?" I shouted, cupping my hands around my mouth.

I pushed open the door. Marissa followed me inside.

We found ourselves in a warm kitchen. Light from a candle on a small table flickered over the wall. I saw a crusty loaf of bread on the sink counter. A carving knife beside it.

I saw a big black pot simmering on a wood-burning stove. It sent a sweet, tangy aroma floating through the room.

I didn't have time to see anything else.

As I took one step into the small kitchen, a figure burst in from a back room.

A very large woman wearing a long, flowing, grey dress.

She had flashing, bright green eyes. A blonde fringe fell across her forehead, and long braids hung down the sides of her round-cheeked face.

She wore a helmet over her head. A cone-shaped helmet with two horns poking up from the sides. Like a Viking from long ago. Or someone in an opera.

Her arms were big, with powerful muscles. She had sparkling rings on every finger. A round, jewelled medallion swung heavily over her chest.

She dashed quickly past Marissa and me, her green eyes wild, her mouth twisted in an evil grin.

She slammed the cabin door shut.

Pressed her back against the door.

"I've *caught* you!" she shrieked. And tossed back her head in an ugly cackle of triumph.

Her cruel laugh ended in a cough. Her green eyes sparkled at us, reflecting the candlelight. She stared at us hungrily.

"Let us go!"

Those were the words I *wanted* to shout.

But when I opened my mouth, only a tiny squeak slipped out.

Marissa moved first. She lunged for the door. I forced my rubbery legs into action, and followed close behind.

"Let us out!" I finally managed to scream. "You can't keep us here!"

The big woman's smile faded. "Take it easy, kids," she boomed. She had a loud, deep voice. "I was just kidding."

Marissa and I both gaped at her. "Excuse me?" I cried.

"Sorry. I have a bad sense of humour," the

woman said. "I guess it comes from living out here in the middle of the forest. I can't resist a really mean joke."

I still didn't understand. "You mean you didn't lock us in?" I demanded in a trembling voice. "You haven't captured us?"

She shook her head. The horns on the helmet moved with her head. She suddenly reminded me of a large, grey bull.

"I haven't captured you. I sent Silverdog so that I could *help* you." She pointed towards the stove.

I saw that the big white dog had dropped down beside it. He lowered his head, licking a big front paw. But he kept his eyes on Marissa and me.

My sister and I stayed near the door. This woman was strange. And kind of terrifying.

She was so big and loud. And powerful-looking. And those green eyes flashed and danced wildly beneath the horned helmet.

Is she totally crazy? I wondered.

Did she really bring us here to help us?

"I know everything that happens in this forest," she said mysteriously. She raised the jewelled medallion close to her face and stared into it. "I have ways of seeing things. Nothing escapes me."

I glanced at Marissa. Her eyes were wide with fright. Her hand reached for the cabin door.

Back by the stove, Silverdog yawned. He lowered his head between his paws.

"What are your names?" the woman boomed. She let the heavy medallion drop back on to her chest. "My name is Ivanna." She narrowed her eyes at me. "Do you know what *Ivanna* means?"

I cleared my throat. "Uh . . . no," I replied.

"I don't, either!" the woman exclaimed. She tossed back her head in another cackling laugh. The medallion bounced on her chest. Her helmet nearly toppled off her blonde hair.

Despite the warmth of the small kitchen, I shivered. We had walked so far through the cold forest. I couldn't shake off the chill.

"You two look half-frozen," Ivanna said, studying our faces. "I think I know what you need. Hot soup. Sit down." She motioned to a small wooden table with two chairs in the corner of the room.

Marissa and I hesitated. I didn't want to leave the door. I knew we were both still thinking of making a run for it.

"Our dad . . ." Marissa murmured. "He'll be looking for us. He might be here—any minute."

Ivanna stepped over to the stove. "Why didn't you bring him along?" she asked. She pulled down two bowls from a cabinet.

"We couldn't wake him up," I blurted out.

Marissa glared at me.

"A heavy sleeper, huh?" Ivanna had her back to us. She was ladling soup from the black pot into the two bowls.

I leaned close to Marissa. "If we want to escape, now is our chance," I whispered.

She turned to the door, then swung back. "I'm so cold," she whispered. "And the soup smells so good."

"Sit down," Ivanna ordered in her deep, booming voice.

I led the way to the small wooden table. Marissa and I sat down on the hard chairs.

Ivanna set the steaming bowls in front of us. Her green eyes lit up as she smiled. "Hot chicken noodle soup. It will warm you and get you ready for your test."

"Huh? Test?" I cried. "What test?"

"Eat. Eat," Ivanna ordered. "Warm yourselves." She stepped back to the stove.

I watched her bend to pet Silverdog's head. Then I raised the soup spoon to my mouth. Blew on it. And swallowed a mouthful.

Delicious.

And it felt so warm and soothing on my dry throat.

I took a few more spoonfuls. Then I glanced across the table. Marissa seemed to be enjoying it too.

I had raised a spoonful of noodles nearly to my mouth—when Ivanna spun towards us from the sink. Her eyes went wide. Her mouth dropped open.

She pointed at us with a trembling finger. "You—you haven't eaten any of it—*have* you?" she demanded.

"Huh?" Marissa and I both gasped.

"Whatever you do, don't eat it!" Ivanna cried. "I—I just remembered. It's *poison!*"

The spoon dropped from my hand and splashed into the bowl. I grabbed my stomach, waiting for the pain to begin.

I glanced over at Marissa—and saw her roll her eyes. "Another joke?" Marissa asked Ivanna.

"Another joke!" Ivanna confessed gleefully. Once again, she roared with laughter.

I swallowed hard. Why didn't I guess it was another one of the woman's mean jokes? I hate it when Marissa catches on to things before I do!

"I knew it all along," I muttered.

Ivanna stepped up to the table, the medallion bouncing as she walked. "The soup isn't poison. But don't eat it yet," she instructed. "I want to read the noodles."

"Excuse me?" I replied.

She leaned over my bowl, bringing her face so close that the steam misted her cheeks.

"Chicken soup noodles foretell your fate," she whispered mysteriously.

She studied the noodles in my bowl. Then she studied Marissa's. "Hmmmm. Hmmmm," she kept repeating. "Yes. Hmmmm hmmmm."

Finally, she stood up and crossed her powerful arms over her chest. Her cheeks were red from the hot steam off the soup.

"Eat. Eat your soup now," she instructed. "Before it gets cold."

"What did you see?" I asked. "In the noodles. What did they tell you?"

Her expression turned solemn. "You must take the test in the morning," she replied. "I was right. I know why you have come to the forest. I know what you seek."

She straightened the helmet on her head. "I can help you. I can help you find it. But first you must take the test."

"Uh . . . what kind of test?" I asked.

Her eyes flashed. "A *survival* test," she replied.

I swallowed hard. "I was afraid of that," I muttered.

"What if we don't *want* to take your survival test?" Marissa demanded.

"Then you will *never* find the silver chest!" Ivanna declared heatedly.

I gasped. "Wow! You *do* know what we're looking for!" I exclaimed.

She nodded. "I know everything in this forest."

"But—but we need our dad!" Marissa stammered.

Ivanna shook her head. "There is no time. You will take the test in his place. Do not worry. It is not a difficult test. If you stay alive."

"Huh? If we *stay alive*? Is that one of your jokes?" I asked weakly.

"No," Ivanna replied, shaking her head. "No joke. I never joke about the test in the Fantasy Forest."

I was holding the soup spoon. But I let it fall to the table. "Fantasy Forest? Where's that? What is it?"

Ivanna opened her mouth to answer. But before she could say a word, the cabin door burst open.

I felt a blast of cold air.

And then a wild creature, covered in black fur, scrabbled into the room on all fours. Snarling, it cast its bulging black eyes around the room.

Then it snapped its jagged teeth—and, with a hoarse growl, leapt to attack me.

I uttered a scream—and tried to dodge out of the way.

My chair fell, and I fell with it.

The chair clattered noisily on to the floorboards. I landed on my side.

I tried to roll away. But the snarling creature sank its teeth into my leg.

"Owwww!" I shrieked.

Over my cry, I heard Ivanna's booming shouts: "Down, Luka! Get down! Off, Luka! Get off!"

The wild creature gurgled. It let go of my leg. And backed away, breathing hard.

As I scrambled to my feet, I stared at the panting creature. It had a man's face. Hunched on its hind legs, it looked almost human. Except that it was covered with thick, black fur.

"Get back, Luka!" Ivanna screamed. "Back!"

The creature obediently inched back.

"Don't be scared of Luka," Ivanna said, turning to me. "He's a good boy."

"What—what *is* he?" I cried, rubbing my leg.

"I'm not sure," Ivanna replied, grinning at the furry thing.

Luka hopped up and down, grinning, making grunting sounds.

"He was brought up by wolves," Ivanna said. "But he's a good boy. Aren't you, Luka?"

Luka nodded. His tongue hung out of his open mouth. He panted like a dog.

Ivanna petted his long, shaggy hair.

He broke away from her and charged at me again. He sniffed my sweatshirt and jeans. Then he crawled under the table and sniffed Marissa's hiking boots.

"Get away, Luka!" Ivanna ordered. "Off! Off!" She turned to me. "He's a good boy. He's just nosy. He'll calm down—once he gets to know you."

"Gets to know us?" Marissa demanded, watching Luka scurry over to Silverdog by the stove.

"Luka will be a big help to you when you enter the Fantasy Forest," Ivanna said with a smile.

"He's coming with us?" I cried.

Ivanna nodded. "He will be your guide. And he will protect you." Her expression turned solemn. Then she added softly, "You need all the help you can get."

We finished our soup quickly. Silverdog and Luka watched us from beside the stove.

When we finished, Ivanna led us to a small back room. The room was bare except for two camp-beds.

"You will sleep here," she said sternly.

"But our dad—" Marissa started.

Ivanna raised a hand to silence her. "You want to find the silver chest—don't you? You want to surprise your father and make him proud—don't you?"

Marissa and I nodded.

"Then you will take the test. If you pass it, I will tell you how to find the chest."

She dropped a coarse wool blanket on to each camp-bed. "Sleep quickly," she instructed. "The test begins first thing in the morning."

I awoke slowly. Stretched. Turned and reached to push the blanket off me.

No blanket.

Had I kicked it on to the floor?

I blinked several times, trying to clear the sleep from my eyes.

How long had I slept?

Sunlight streamed all around.

Yawning, I sat up. Started to climb off the camp-bed.

But the camp-bed had disappeared, too.

"Hey—!" I cried out when I realized the cabin had also disappeared.

"Where am I?"

I was sitting on the grass, fully dressed. I blinked, waiting for my eyes to adjust to the bright morning sunlight. The grass still shimmered wetly from the morning dew.

I stood up. My mouth dry. Feeling stunned.

Nothing but forest all around.

My mind whirled. Ivanna had said the test would begin first thing in the morning.

Had it already begun? Was I in the Fantasy Forest?

Had the test begun *before* I awoke?

Rubbing my eyes, I turned to Marissa. "Where are we?" I asked, my voice still hoarse from sleep. I cleared my throat. "Do you think—"

I stopped with a gasp when I realized Marissa wasn't there.

I was alone.

Alone in the middle of the forest.

"Marissa—?" I called, feeling the panic tighten my chest. Where *was* she?

Where was *I*?

"Marissa—? Marissa—?"

"Marissa—?"

My voice cracked. My throat tightened.

I heard a low growl from the trees. The thud and crackle of heavy animal footsteps.

I turned to the sound. And watched Luka come hopping out of the forest. He stood on his two feet like a man. But he hopped like a rabbit. Scratching the thick fur on one leg, he grinned at me as he came near.

I didn't grin back. "Where is Marissa?" I demanded. "Where is my sister?"

He tilted his head and stared at me, confused.

"Marissa!" I screamed at him. "Where is Marissa?"

"Over here!"

I jumped when her voice leapt out at me. "Where are you?" I called.

I saw a flash of her red hair. Then she poked her head out from behind a wide, leafy bush.

"Over here," she repeated. "You were still asleep. So I thought I'd explore."

"You scared me to death!" I admitted. I began trotting through the tall grass and weeds, eager to join her. "Where are we?" I demanded. "What happened to Ivanna's cabin?"

Marissa shrugged. "Beats me. I woke up—and here we were."

Behind us, Luka growled.

I turned and saw him pawing the dirt, like a dog. "Do you think he's part human?" I whispered to Marissa.

She didn't seem to hear me. She pointed to a spot between two trees. "I found a path over there. Do you think we're supposed to follow it?"

"I don't know *what* we're supposed to do," I replied shrilly. "Did Ivanna ever explain the test? No. Did she ever tell us the rules? No. Did she ever tell us what we're supposed to do to *pass* the test? No."

Marissa's eyes narrowed in fear. "I think we're supposed to stay alive," she said softly. "I think that's how we pass the test."

"But where do we go? What do we do?" I cried. I could feel myself start to lose control. I felt angry and frightened and confused—all at the same time.

Luka uttered another growl. He stopped digging up the dirt and came staggering over to us, standing up like a human.

If he shaved off all the fur, put on some clothes, and got a haircut, he'd look like a young man, I thought. As I stared at him, he started to wave and point.

"What is he doing?" I asked Marissa.

She stepped up beside me and stared at him too.

Luka grunted excitedly. He waved a furry hand at us and jabbed his other hand towards the trees.

"I think he wants us to follow him," I said.

"Yes," Marissa agreed. "Remember—Ivanna said he would be our guide."

Grunting and waving, Luka headed for the trees.

I held back. "Can we trust him?" I asked.

Marissa shrugged. "Do we have a choice?"

Luka stepped on to a path that led through the forest. The path curved behind a clump of tall, yellow-leafed bushes. I saw his head bobbing above the bushes. Then he disappeared.

"Hurry!" I tugged my sister's arm. "We'd better not let him get out of sight."

I glanced down and saw two black rucksacks on the grass. I bent down, grabbed one, and unzipped it. Empty.

I handed the other rucksack to Marissa. "Ivanna must have left these for us," I told her. "They're empty. But I guess we should take them."

We pulled the rucksacks on to our backs. Then we jogged to the path and hurried to catch up with the bouncing, hopping Luka.

He stopped to sniff a weed. Then he continued shuffling along the path.

We followed close behind. Two or three times, he turned back to make sure we were following.

The path curved between prickly weeds and tall reeds. We passed a small, round pond that reflected the blue sky. The air became warmer and wet. The back of my neck felt hot and prickly.

We entered a cluster of trees with smooth, white trunks. The trees grew close together. The smooth bark of the trunks felt cool against my hot hands.

"Where is he taking us?" Marissa whispered.

I didn't answer her. I didn't know. I only knew that Luka was leading us deeper and deeper into this forest.

We squeezed our way through the white-trunked trees. And came out in a large, grassy clearing. Small grey rocks poked up from the grass. The slender white trees formed a circle around the clearing.

My boots crunched over the ground as I followed Luka across the grass. I looked down to see what made the crunching sound.

And discovered that the ground was covered with large brown nuts.

I picked one up. "Check this out," I called to Marissa. I turned and saw that she had picked up two of them. "They must have fallen off the white trees," I said.

"They look like walnuts. But they're bigger than eggs!" she declared. "I've never seen walnuts this big!"

"They feel so hot!" I exclaimed. I glanced up at the sky. "I guess it's from the sun beating down on them."

"Hey—! Whoa!"

Marissa's cry made me look up.

I saw a grey creature scamper across the clearing.

At first I thought it was a dog or a very large cat. Then I realized it was a squirrel. It carried one of the large nuts in its front paws. And it hopped quickly towards the trees, its bushy grey tail floating behind it like a pennant.

I turned as Luka let out a hoarse cry.

I saw him stand straight up. I saw his eyes go wide with excitement.

He let out another cry. Leaned forward. Reached out both hands.

And started to chase after the squirrel.

The squirrel saw Luka coming. It dropped the nut and took off at full speed into the white trees.

Luka dropped to all fours and galloped after it.

"No, Luka—come back!" Marissa shouted.

"Come back! Come back!" we both called. "Luka—come back!"

Marissa and I both let out worried cries. Then we took off after Luka, into the clump of trees.

"Luka—! Hey, Luka!" I called. My voice bounced off the trees. It echoed all around me.

"Luka—! Hey, Luka!"

The cry repeated and repeated, echoing loudly.

I could hear his growl up ahead. And I could hear him thrashing his way through the trees as he chased the fat squirrel.

"Luka—come back!" Marissa's cry echoed all around the forest, too.

As we called after him, it sounded as if there were *dozens* of us in the forest, all chasing after him, all frantically calling for him to stop chasing that squirrel and come back to us.

"Whoa!" I cried out as I tried to slip through the narrow space between two white tree trunks— and my rucksack caught between the trees.

"Ow!"

It snapped me back. I staggered and nearly fell.

Mister Klutz. For a change.

"Luka! Hey—Luka!" I could hear Marissa's cry up ahead of me now.

I tried to slip through the trees again, and the rucksack caught again. I pulled it free and found another, wider opening.

A few seconds later, I caught up with my sister. She had stopped running. She leaned against a tree trunk, breathing hard.

"Where is he?" I cried. "Can you see him? Where did he go?"

"I—I lost him," Marissa replied breathlessly. "I can't even hear him any more."

I listened hard. The forest was silent now. No footsteps. No growls. The leaves above us brushed together, making a soft, whispering sound.

"But how could he run away?" I cried. "He's supposed to be our guide!"

"I think he really wanted to catch that squirrel," Marissa said quietly.

"But—but—" I sputtered. "He can't just run away and leave us all by ourselves here."

Marissa sighed. "I think he just did."

"We have to find him!" I cried. "Come on. We have to keep going. We can't let him—"

Marissa shook her head. "How can we find him, Justin? Which way should we go?"

"We'll follow his footprints," I replied. I lowered my gaze to the ground. A thick carpet of brown leaves spread over the dirt.

No footprints.

"I think he was heading that way," I said, pointing to the trees.

Marissa shook her head. "I don't think so." She pushed herself away from the tree trunk. "He's gone, Justin."

I spun around, frantically searching for him. For any sign of him.

"Hey—what's that?" Marissa called.

"Huh?" I turned back to her.

"In your back pocket," she said, pointing. "What is it?"

Confused, I reached into the back pocket of my jeans—and pulled out a folded-up sheet of paper. My hands were sweaty and stuck to the paper. But I unfolded it quickly.

"It's some kind of a note," I told Marissa. "In tiny handwriting."

"Well, *read* it!" she cried.

My eyes slid to the bottom of the page. "It—it's from Ivanna," I stammered excitedly.

"What does it say?" Marissa demanded impatiently.

I steadied the page between both my hands and read the note out loud to both of us:

"DEAR KIDS,

KEEP LUKA WITH YOU, AND YOU WILL PASS THE TEST. DO NOT LET HIM OUT OF YOUR SIGHT. BE CAREFUL NOT TO LOSE HIM—OR YOU ARE DOOMED."

Marissa and I made our way slowly back to the clearing. The grass swayed under a soft breeze. Our boots crunched over the large nuts in the grass.

I still held Ivanna's note in my hand. I glanced over it one more time, hoping it didn't say what it said. Then I angrily balled it up and tossed it away.

Marissa trudged along beside me. The sun beat down on us. We were both sweating.

"Maybe if we wait here, Luka will come back," Marissa said.

"He isn't coming back," I groaned. "He is probably miles away, still chasing after that squirrel."

"Then what do we do next?" Marissa demanded. "How do we pass the test?"

I let out an unhappy sigh. "We *can't* pass the test. You heard what the note said. We're doomed."

"Well, we can *try*," she insisted. She started across the clearing. I followed her.

We had taken six or seven steps when I heard a startling sound. A loud *snap*, like a pencil being broken in two.

Then a *crack*—soft at first, and then louder.

I stopped and whirled around. I expected to see Luka come bounding out of the forest.

But I saw only the tall, white trees. No one there.

I heard another sharp *snap*. Then another. And another.

And then I heard cracking all around.

The earth is cracking open!

That was my first thought. I pictured the ground splitting apart. A dark hole opening up. And Marissa and me falling, falling down into it.

The Pit With No Bottom!

I wished Dad had never told us that story!

Now Marissa grabbed my shoulder and pointed down. "Justin—look!"

I gazed down. The ground hadn't split open. But the snapping and cracking echoed all around.

Louder. Louder.

"Ohh!" I let out a frightened moan as I realized to my horror that the grass was moving.

I could feel it move under my feet.

"What's *happening*?" Marissa cried, still holding on to me. "That sound—!"

The cracking grew louder, rising up from the ground. Now it sounded as if all the trees were cracking apart.

The grass swayed and bent.

"It's—the nuts!" I cried to Marissa. "Look! They're all cracking open!"

I covered my ears against the sound.

And stared at the nuts, bouncing and trembling all around our feet.

Cracking open. Splitting apart.

Hundreds and hundreds of them. The whole clearing. The ground shaking as they all cracked apart.

Cracked into pieces. Crumbled around us.

We stared in amazement at the cracking nuts. And then, Marissa and I both screamed in shock when we saw what came climbing out.

Staring down as a nut split open, I saw gnashing teeth. Tiny black eyes. A twitching black nose.

The creature pushed itself up. I saw spindly front legs.

A slender body of grey fur.

And those teeth. Snapping. Gnashing.

"A mouse!" I choked out.

"Hundreds of them!" Marissa cried.

The nuts were splitting apart. All across the clearing. So many of them, it made the grass quiver and the ground appear to shake.

I stood frozen in place, watching mice hatch around my feet. They pushed out slowly, poking their heads out first. Sniffing the air. Trying out their pointy teeth.

The nuts rocked on to their sides. Cracked apart. Grey bodies slithered out. Sticklike back legs kicked their way out from the empty shells.

"They're not nuts—they're eggs!" Marissa wailed.

187

"But mice don't come from eggs!" I protested.

Marissa raised her eyes to me, her face twisted in shock. "I guess no one told these mice!"

A mouse scampered over my boots. Mice were scurrying through the tall grass, making the grass whisper.

Another grey body slithered over my boots.

"Let's get *out* of here!" I cried to Marissa. I grabbed her arm and started to pull.

But so many mice scampered over the grass, so many grey bodies slithered at our feet—we couldn't move.

Shrill squeaks rose up from the grass as the creatures found their voices. "*Eee eee eee eee!*" The sound surrounded us. Grew louder, louder. Until it drowned out the whisper of the grass. Until it forced Marissa and me to cover our ears.

"*Eee eee eee eee!*"

"We have to *run!*" I shouted.

"But the ground is covered!" Marissa shrieked. "If we run—"

"YOWWWWW!" I let out a cry as I felt a mouse drop inside my hiking boot. Its tiny feet scratched through my wool socks.

I bent down to pull it out—and saw two more mice clinging by their teeth to my trouser leg.

"Hey—" I tried to bat them away.

Lost my balance.

Fell to my knees.

188

Justin the Super Klutz strikes again.

Mice scurried over my hands. I felt one climb up my sweatshirt sleeve, on to my back.

"Hellllp!" Marissa and I both cried out at the same time.

I turned and saw her bent over, hands raised, struggling to pull two mice from her hair.

Another mouse chewed the bottom of her sweatshirt. Two more mice climbed a leg of her jeans. Mice clung to her rucksack.

"Helllp me! Ohhhh—helllp!"

Still on my knees, I struggled to push myself up. But a mouse slithered under my sweatshirt. I felt its prickly feet move across my chest. Then I felt a sharp stab of pain in the middle of my back.

Did it *bite* me?

Mice jumped on to my shoulders. Crawled over the back of my neck. Swarmed over my rucksack.

Swinging both hands wildly, I tried to brush them off me.

But there were too many of them.

Squeaking. Snapping. Clinging to my clothes. My wrists. My hair.

"Hellllp! Helllp!"

I pulled a mouse from my ear. And tossed it across the grass.

I could feel a bunch of them crawling over my bare skin under my sweatshirt. Another sharp bite made me cry out—and I dropped face down on to the grass—on to more mice!

I tried to swat the mice away. Tried to swat them and push them and grab them and tug them off me.

But there were too many. Far too many.

I turned and saw them swarming over Marissa. She cried out as she spun around, swinging her arms. Trying to shake the mice off.

I wanted to help her. But I couldn't get up.

My whole body tingled and itched.

The squeaking, chattering mice swarmed over me, holding me down. Prickling me, scratching me, biting me—until I couldn't move, couldn't breathe.

"Off! Get off!" I managed to cry.

I swiped at my face, slapping two mice off my cheeks. I pulled one, squeaking and squirming, from my hair. Pulled another one off my forehead.

I kicked my legs and swung my arms, frantically trying to free myself.

"Oww!" I let out a wild shriek as a fat, grey mouse scratched at my ear.

I reached up. Grabbed it. And squeezed.

The mouse gave a soft groan—and collapsed.

"Huh?" I felt something hard above its furry grey belly. Like a bump.

I slapped away two other mice and examined the one in my hand. I pushed the tiny, hard bump. The mouse started to squirm and struggle.

I pushed the bump again. The mouse slumped in my hand, silent and still.

"It's an on–off switch!" I screamed.

I turned to Marissa. She had fallen to her knees. Dozens of mice swarmed over her. They covered her sweatshirt. They crawled through her hair.

"It's an on–off switch!" I shouted to her. "Marissa—squeeze the button on their front. You can turn them off!"

I grabbed a mouse off my neck. Squeezed the button. Shut it off.

I swiped up two more and turned them off.

"They're not real!" I cried happily. "The mice—they're fakes! They're little machines!"

Marissa climbed to her feet. She was brushing mice off her clothes. Clicking them off. "Weird!" she exclaimed. "Justin—this is so weird!"

"We've got to get out of here," I told her. "We've got to find Luka."

Marissa tugged a mouse off the back of her neck and clicked it off. "Do you think this was the test?" she asked. "Do you think we passed it?"

"I don't know," I replied. My eyes searched the trees. "I don't care about the test right now. I just want to get away from these stupid mechanical mice."

I brushed two more off the front of my jeans. Then I reached for Marissa. I pulled a mouse off her shoulder, clicked it off, and tossed it away.

Then we both started to run for the trees.

Mice scurried under our feet. Their shrill squeaks echoed all around us.

We stepped on them as we ran. But we didn't care. We knew they weren't real. We knew they were mechanical.

We were nearly out of the clearing when I stopped suddenly. I had an idea.

I bent down and started scooping up mice. "Wait up!" I called to Marissa.

She didn't hear me. She kept running towards the trees.

"Wait up! I'll be right there!" I called. I picked up a few handfuls of mice and clicked them off. Then I shoved them into my rucksack.

These will be *awesome* for playing jokes on people back home! I told myself. They're so life-like. Can you imagine the fun I'll have with these in Miss Olsen's class?

I shoved eight or nine more of them into the pack and closed it up. Then I climbed to my feet and ran after my sister.

I glanced back once—and saw the mice, thousands of them, crawling over each other, crawling in wild circles through the grass.

Then I turned and ran, following Marissa into the safety of the white-trunked trees. Ran full-speed. Ran blindly.

So eager to get away from that clearing and the squeaking, scurrying mice.

"Marissa—wait up!" I called.

She was far ahead, running fast.

"Wait up!" I called.

And then I uttered a sharp cry as I ran—full-force—into a tree.

"Oooof!"

I felt the air burst from my lungs. I saw stars. Red and yellow stars, dancing in a pure white sky.

Gasping for breath, I reached for the tree trunk.

I heard a cracking sound.

So loud. And close.

The tree!

The tree I had run into—it started to fall!

"Look out—!" I called to my sister.

Too late.

As I stared helplessly, the tall, white tree collapsed.

Marissa's hands shot up as the tree fell on her.

And crushed her beneath its heavy trunk.

"Nooooo!" I let out a howl of horror. And stared down at my sister.

Marissa lay sprawled face down in the dirt. The tree trunk had crushed her back and shoulders.

Was she breathing?

I couldn't tell.

"Marissa—!" I choked out her name and dropped down beside her. "I—I—"

I saw her body give a hard shake.

She raised her head and squinted up at me. "What happened?" Her words came out in a whisper.

"Does it hurt?" I cried. "Are you in pain?"

She squinted harder, as if thinking about it. "No. No pain." Marissa rolled on to her back. Then she reached up with both hands—and shoved the tree trunk off her.

"Huh?" I let out a startled cry.

I saw the bewildered expression on my sister's face. "It's fake too," she murmured.

She reached out and tugged off a chunk of the tree trunk. "It's plaster or something," she announced. "Check it out, Justin."

My hand was trembling as I tore off a piece of the trunk. I was still shaking all over from the sight of Marissa falling under the tree.

I squeezed the chunk of tree, and it turned to powder in my hand. I pulled off another hunk. Soft plaster.

Marissa climbed to her feet. She brushed the plaster dust off her clothes. "It's a total fake," she murmured again.

"Do you think *all* the trees are fake?" I cried. "The whole forest?"

I got up. Then I took a running start. Stuck both hands straight out in front of me . . .

. . . And ran as hard as I could, shoving my hands against a tree.

The trunk cracked easily. I stood shaking my head in amazement as the tree toppled over. It hit another tree and knocked that one down too. The plaster trunks cracked and shattered as they hit the ground.

"Fake. It's all fake!" Marissa declared. A smile spread over her face. "That looks like fun."

She took a running start, aiming at a tree across from the others.

"No! Not that one!" I screamed.

I guess Marissa couldn't stop in time. She slammed her shoulder into the tree. "Yaaaay!" She raised both fists over her head in triumph as the tree toppled over.

But she didn't have much time to cheer.

As the white trunk fell, I heard the hard flutter of wings.

And I watched in horror as dark forms fluttered up from the fallen branches.

I had seen the bats. Dozens of black bats. Clinging upside down on the tree.

I had seen them. But I hadn't warned Marissa in time.

And now the bats all came flapping up, chittering angrily, their sleep interrupted.

Hissing and shrieking at us, they surrounded us—and began to circle. I could feel the warm breeze from their flapping wings.

Faster. Faster, they circled.

"Are they fake too?" Marissa asked in a tiny voice.

"I—I don't think so," I stammered as they swooped in for the kill.

197

21

Marissa and I both ducked as the circle of bats swooped low.

I shut my eyes and covered my head with my hands.

And waited.

The sound of a deep *boom* rose over the shrill chittering of the bats.

The ground shook.

Thunder?

Another boom, low at first, then loud as an explosion.

I raised my head in time to see the white trees tremble.

The bats stopped their shrieking. Their wings shot up, stretched out.

Another boom of thunder sent them racing back up to the sky. I watched them flutter up, rising, rising above the trees, rising against the bright sky until they seemed to disappear into the sun.

Marissa let out a long sigh of relief. "We're safe." She climbed to her feet slowly.

"But what is that sound?" I demanded, listening hard.

Another thunderous *boom*. Closer this time.

I felt the ground shake. A tree tottered, then came toppling to the ground.

"It can't be thunder," Marissa said softly. She pointed to the sky. "No clouds or anything."

Another *boom*.

Closer.

"I—I know what it is," I stammered.

Marissa turned to me. Another *boom* shook the trees.

"Footsteps," I murmured. "Coming towards us. I know it's footsteps."

Marissa's mouth dropped open. "Justin— you're letting your crazy imagination run away with you. Again!"

"No. I'm right," I insisted. "Footsteps."

My sister squinted at me. "Are you going mad? What could make footsteps that loud? It would have to be . . ." Her voice trailed off.

Another *boom*.

I let my crazy imagination run away with me. I couldn't help it. I pictured a dinosaur. A Tyrannosaurus rex. Lumbering through the trees. Or maybe one of those fat ones with the long, skinny necks.

Boooooom. Booooom.

Or maybe *two* of them!

"Whatever it is, it's coming closer," Marissa whispered. She shook her head. "Ivanna *said* this was a test of survival. But—"

So far, it had been a test of our *running skills*!

But I didn't care. There was no way I wanted to stick around to see what this giant creature was.

As Marissa and I turned and started to run in the opposite direction, a shadow fell over us.

I gazed up to see if clouds had blocked the sun.

But I saw no clouds overhead.

The shadow was cast by the creature, thundering closer and closer behind us.

I heard trees crunching underfoot. The ground shook. The heavy footsteps boomed close behind us.

How tall *was* it?

I glanced back—but could see only quivering trees.

Boooooom. Booooom.

My knees buckled as the ground shook under my feet.

Marissa and I ran side by side. We hurtled through the trees as fast as we could, gasping for breath as we ran.

But we couldn't run out of the shadow. No matter how hard we ran, it floated over us, cold and dark.

Booooom. Booooom.

So close now. So close that every footstep made me leap into the air.

My heart thudded. My temples throbbed.

Marissa and I forced ourselves to keep running, desperate to escape, desperate to run out from under the wide shadow that seemed to hold us prisoner.

We ran until we reached a wide stream.

We both stopped centimetres from the muddy shore. And stared down into the fast-flowing, blue water.

"Now what?" I cried breathlessly. "Now what?"

The shadow darkened as the creature moved over us.

Marissa tugged my sleeve. "Look. You can see the bottom. It looks really shallow. Maybe we can walk across it. Or swim if we have to."

Boooom. Boooom.

The shadow darkened.

"Let's go," I said.

We stepped into the cold, clear stream.

The water flowed faster than I thought. I stepped on to the stream's soft bottom—and nearly lost my balance as the current swept around me.

I grabbed Marissa's shoulder to steady myself. We clung together for a moment, getting used to the water.

"Brrrr." I shivered. The water felt ice cold, even through my jeans legs.

But it was shallow, as Marissa had said. It came up only a few centimetres above my boots.

I took another step, leaning forward, trying to balance against the stream's fast current.

One more step. We were both halfway across the stream.

"Oh—!" I cried out when I realized I couldn't take the next step.

"Hey—!" Marissa exclaimed. I saw her struggling, too. "I'm stuck!"

"The bottom is so soft!" I cried. I worked to pull my foot up from the mud.

Stuck. My hiking boots had sunk below the surface of the muddy bottom.

I leaned down. And pulled. Pulled my leg up. It wouldn't budge.

I grabbed my leg with both hands and tried to tug my foot out from the muddy stream bottom. No.

"We—we're sinking!" Marissa wailed. "Justin—look! We're sinking fast!"

I swallowed hard. She was right. I could feel myself being pulled down. Down into the cold water, into the soft, sticky mud.

The water came up to my knees now. It seemed to be rising quickly.

But I knew the water wasn't going up. I was heading *down*.

"Pull off your boots and swim for it!" I instructed Marissa.

We both bent over and struggled to reach our hiking boots.

But they were buried too deeply in the mud.

The water rose up over my waist. If I kept sinking, it would be over my head in a few minutes.

Booom. Booom.

The thundering footsteps made the water ripple.

The dark shadow spread over the stream.

"Justin—look!" Marissa cried. She pointed to the other shore.

I turned to the shore—so close. But so far away.

I squinted into the shadows to see what she was gawking at. "What is it?" I cried.

"A big plug," Marissa reported. "In the stream bottom. Like the plug-hole in a bath. This stream isn't real, either. It's a fake."

"The water feels real enough!" I exclaimed, feeling myself sink even deeper into the mud. "Can you reach the plug, Marissa? Maybe if you pull it up, the water will drain away."

She leaned towards it, bending at the waist. She stretched out both hands for the ring on top of the plug. "I–I'm trying," she groaned. "If only . . ."

Boooom. Booooom.

Marissa uttered a sigh. "I can't! I can't reach it! It's too far away."

The cold stream water flowed against my chest. I felt myself drop further into the muddy bottom.

"I think we've failed Ivanna's test," I murmured.

"Noooo!" Marissa wailed. She began thrashing at the water with both hands, twisting her body one way, then the other.

The deepening shadow moved over us.

I turned back and raised my eyes to the shore.

I saw the creatures lurching towards us.
And opened my mouth in an ear-shattering scream of horror.

At first I thought I was seeing black clouds, floating low over the trees.

But then I realized the bobbing shapes were too dark to be clouds. Too dark and too solid.

And then I saw the twin pairs of yellow eyes.

And I recognized the shapes of the heads. And I knew I was staring at cats.

Cats!

Black cats. Huge heads rising over the trees. Tails curling up like smoke from chimneys.

Two giant black cats, their paws thundering over the forest, shaking the ground and the trees. Their yellow eyes locked on Marissa and me.

"They're ... not real!" Marissa murmured. "Not real ... not real." She had stopped thrashing the water and stood now perfectly still, staring back at the enormous cats, repeating the words like a chant.

Trees crunched and fell. The two cats thundered their way to the shore.

"Noooo . . ." A low wail escaped Marissa's throat.

I struggled to breathe. My chest ached. My head started to spin.

The cats pulled back their lips in a terrifying hiss.

I saw rows of sharp teeth. I saw their yellow eyes narrow menacingly.

Tossing back their heads in another hiss, the creatures arched their backs. The black fur on their backs stood straight up.

"Wh-what are they going to do?" Marissa stammered.

I opened my mouth to answer her, but only a tiny squeak escaped.

The water flowed past my shoulders. I raised my hands out of the water, trying to keep from sinking under.

"Justin—what are they going to *do*?" she repeated in a shriek.

We didn't have to wait long to find out.

Before we could even cry out, the cat heads came swooping down at us. The jaws opened wide. The curled and jagged teeth slid apart.

I turned and tried to squirm and wriggle away. But I couldn't move. Water splashed over my face. Then I felt teeth clamp shut on the back of my sweatshirt.

Sputtering, gasping for breath, I felt myself lifted up. My boots made a popping sound as they were pulled from the mud.

I felt the cat's hot breath on my neck and the back of my head. The teeth held me firmly, plucking me up, up out of the stream.

"Whoooooa!" I finally found my voice.

The cat dangled me high in the air.

My arms and legs thrashed wildly. The cat tossed its head, swinging me from side to side.

"Helllp! Ohhh, help!" I heard my sister's cry from nearby. I turned and saw her hoisted up by the other cat, hoisted high in the air, the cat's jaws clamped tightly on the back of Marissa's sweatshirt.

I tried to call out to Marissa. But a burst of hot cat breath nearly suffocated me.

I felt myself being lifted even higher as the cat rose up on its hind legs. A paw swung up and batted my side. The other paw batted me the other way.

Does it think I'm a cat toy? I wondered.

I didn't have time to think about it.

I twisted dizzily as the cat played with me, batting me from side to side. Then, suddenly, I found myself being lowered.

The jaws opened.

I was falling now.

Into the water?

No. I landed hard on my back on the shore.

So hard, I bounced. Pain shot through my body.

I ignored it and scrambled to my feet. My heart pounding, my whole body shaking, I tried to run.

But the cat grabbed me up again, its jaws closing around my right shoulder.

As I sailed back up into the air, I saw Marissa falling through the air. I heard her cry out as she hit the ground. And then I saw the other black cat bend its head, open its jaws, and drag Marissa up in the air again.

Up—and then down. My body slammed hard on the shore. I gasped and struggled to my hands and knees. In time to be picked up again and dangled over the water.

Marissa and I both hung over the stream.

Then once more, we were dropped to the shore.

"Oww!" I bounced hard. Stared up as the cat lowered its massive head to pick me up again.

"What are they *doing*?" Marissa screeched. "Why are they *doing* this?"

"I know what they're doing. They're doing what cats always do!" I cried, feeling cold horror run down my body. "They're playing with their food."

"Whooooaaa!"

My stomach lurched as I felt myself being swooped up into the air again. A black cat's paw swiped at me and sent me swinging.

"They—they're going to *eat* us?" Marissa called.

"We must look like mice to them!" I shouted back.

And then I had an idea.

The cat tossed its head and sent me flying. It caught me between its enormous paws. The paws squeezed my middle so hard, I thought my head might pop off!

But as I struggled to breathe, my idea gave me hope.

Do I have time? I wondered. *Can I do it—before this cat swallows me whole?*

The cat tossed me up again, then caught me between its teeth. Pain shot down my back. My whole body tingled and ached.

With a groan, I twisted my body. I reached behind me and struggled to grab the rucksack.

If I can unzip it, I thought, maybe I can reach the mechanical mice I'd stuffed inside. And maybe I can switch one or two of them on. And maybe the mice will distract the two cats. And maybe Marissa and I can escape.

Maybe, maybe, maybe.

But I *had* to try something. Or else in a few seconds, Marissa and I would be cat food.

The cat's tongue swept over the back of my neck. I cried out in pain. The tongue felt as rough as sandpaper! Hot cat breath stung my neck.

I grabbed the rucksack with one hand and started to tug it around to my chest.

But the cat opened its jaws. The rough tongue bumped me from behind. And I went flying back to the ground.

I landed hard on my hands and knees. Pain shot through me once again. I felt like collapsing in the dirt.

But I knew I couldn't give up.

The cat leaned over me, hissing each breath. Yellow eyes gleamed down at me hungrily.

Ignoring the pain, I grabbed the rucksack. I pulled the straps off my shoulder. Then I swung the pack around to my chest and gripped it tightly with both hands.

"Got to get the mice," I murmured out loud.

"Got to get the kitty cat some mice to play with."

My hands were trembling so hard, I couldn't work the zip.

"Aaaaagh!" I let out a frustrated cry—just as the cat swooped me up in its jaws again.

I tried to call out to Marissa. I wanted to tell her to hold on. That I had a plan.

High in the air, I gripped the rucksack with my right hand. Reached for the zip with my left.

Please. Please! I prayed silently. Let me get the mice out. Let me click them on.

"My only chance," I muttered, struggling with the rucksack zip. "My only chance . . ."

A burst of hot cat breath made me shudder. Once again I felt the dry, scratchy tongue scrape the back of my neck.

"Yessss!" I shouted as I finally pulled the zip and opened the rucksack.

"Yessss!"

I shot my hand excitedly into the rucksack. I felt the furry mechanical creatures inside.

I started to wrap my fingers around one . . .

But the cat swung me hard. Tossed back its head and flung me into the air.

"Noooooo!" I let out a long wail—and felt the rucksack fly out of my hands.

"Noooooo!" I frantically grabbed at it. Grabbed with both hands. Missed. Then I tried to snare it on my foot.

"Noooooo!" I watched the rucksack sail to the ground.

It bounced once. Twice. Then lay in the dirt near the shore.

The cat caught me in its teeth. I felt the sharp points dig into my skin.

Then the jaws opened. And I started to slide. Down the scratchy tongue. Down, down into the cat's cavern of a mouth.

"Sorry, Marissa," I murmured in my panic. "We are doomed."

The ground disappeared from view as I slid further down the cat's rough tongue. On my stomach, I reached out with both hands.

And grabbed the two curved eyeteeth. They felt warm and sticky in my hands.

With a hard tug, I pulled myself part of the way up. I crawled a little way on the tongue. Then I gave another tug, and my head poked out from the cat's open mouth.

I searched for Marissa, but I couldn't see her.

Had she already been swallowed?

Beneath me, the tongue bucked and curled. The cat was trying to force me down.

But I held tightly on to the eyeteeth. And glimpsed the ground far below.

And saw three or four grey mice scampering out of the rucksack, on to the dirt.

They must have clicked on when the rucksack hit the ground!

Would the cats see them? Would they *care*?

The cat chomped its teeth together. I cried out in pain, and my hands slid off the eyeteeth.

The tongue rolled beneath me. I started to slide again.

The mouth closed over me, shutting me in darkness. "Ohhhh." So hot and wet inside. So hard to breathe.

I heard low gurgling and growling below me in the cat's stomach.

"No!" I cried. "No no no no!" My voice sounded tiny and muffled inside the cat's mouth.

And then, to my shock, the sunlight poured back in as the jaws popped open.

The tongue pushed me forward. Past the teeth. Past the lips.

I sucked in a deep breath of cool, fresh air.

And then I went flying from the cat's mouth.

I landed on my back on the ground next to Marissa. She gaped at me in surprise, her eyes wild, her red hair tangled and matted wetly to her head.

We both scrambled to our feet—in time to see both giant black cats pounce.

They both leapt at the same mechanical mouse.

Hissing and clawing at each other, they began to fight over it.

"Marissa—let's go!" I choked out.

She stared in amazement as the giant cats

wrestled, hissing and scratching, rolling into the stream, then out again.

"Hurry! Let's go!" I shouted. I grabbed Marissa with both hands and tugged. "If they figure out the mice aren't real, they'll come back after us!"

"But are the *cats* real?" Marissa demanded, still gazing at them in amazement. "Are the cats real? Or fake?"

"*Who cares?*" I shrieked. "Let's get *out* of here!"

Once again, we started running through the forest. Which way were we going? We didn't pay any attention. We just wanted to get as far away from those cats as we could.

My clothes felt wet and sticky from the inside of the cat's mouth. But the cool, fresh air felt good against my skin and helped to dry me off.

Our shadows leaned ahead of us, as if leading the way. I heard strange animal calls that sounded like shrill laughter. And I heard the flapping of wings above the trees.

But Marissa and I ignored all the sounds. We kept running, pushing tall weeds and shrubs out of our way, making our own path.

We didn't speak. We didn't even look at each other. We ran side by side, keeping each other in sight, helping each other through the tangled forest.

We were both breathless when we reached a

round, grassy clearing. White and yellow moths floated silently over the swaying grass.

"Marissa—look!" I gasped, pointing to the other side of the clearing.

A small cabin stood under the trees where the grass ended. A very familiar cabin.

"It's Ivanna's!" Marissa exclaimed happily. "Justin—we made it! We're back!"

I sucked in a deep breath and scrambled across the grass. Marissa ran right behind me.

"Ivanna! Ivanna!" We both called her name as we hurried to the cabin.

She didn't come out. So I grabbed the door and pushed it open. "Ivanna—we're back!" I cried happily. I glanced quickly around the room, waiting for my eyes to adjust to the dim light.

Marissa pushed me aside as she burst into the small kitchen. "We survived!" she exclaimed. "Ivanna—is the test over? Did we pass it? Justin and I—"

We both saw Ivanna seated at the small wooden table. She sat stooped over, her head on the table.

Her horned helmet had fallen off. It lay on its side on the table. Her long blonde braids had come undone and fallen over her face.

"Ivanna? Ivanna?" I called. I turned to my sister. "She must be asleep."

"Ivanna?" Marissa called. "We're back!"

The woman didn't stir.

I heard a whimper from the back of the room. Squinting into the shadows, I saw Silverdog. He was huddled sadly against the wall, his head on the floor between his paws. He let out another whimper.

"Justin—something is wrong here," Marissa whispered.

"Ivanna! Ivanna!" I shouted her name. But she still didn't move.

The big white dog whimpered sadly.

"Is she asleep?" Marissa demanded. "What's *wrong* with her?"

"Let's see," I murmured.

I took a deep breath and made my way across the kitchen to the table. Marissa raised her hands to her cheeks and stared at me. She didn't budge.

I was nearly to the table when I stopped with a gasp.

"Wh-what's wrong?" Marissa stammered.

"Look what's sticking out of her back!" I choked out.

"Huh?" Marissa's mouth dropped open in horror. "Justin—what?"

I swallowed hard. My legs started to tremble. I grabbed the back of a chair to steady myself.

"Marissa—look," I instructed, still pointing.

She came a couple of steps closer, her eyes bulging wide with fear.

We both stared at the metal object poking out from the back of Ivanna's dress.

A large metal key.

I worked up my courage and crept up behind Ivanna. My heart pounding, I leaned down and examined the big key.

"It—it's a *wind-up* key!" I stammered.

Marissa opened her mouth, but no sound came out.

I took the key in both hands and turned it one click.

Ivanna's head bobbed up, then fell back to the table.

"Yes. It's a wind-up key," I told my sister.

Ivanna's hands had dropped to the floor at her sides. I reached down and grabbed one of them.

It felt soft and spongy. Stuffed with cotton or something.

I let the hand drop to the floor and turned back to Marissa. "Ivanna isn't real," I told her, swallowing again. "She's some kind of dummy or puppet or something. Ivanna isn't real, either!"

"Then what *is* real?" Marissa demanded in a tiny voice. "This is so scary, Justin. Is it all part of a test, or what? How do we get out of here now? How do we find Dad? If Ivanna isn't real, then who is?"

I just shook my head. I didn't know how to answer her questions. I felt as frightened as she did.

My eyes fell on Silverdog back in the corner. The dog had his head buried in his paws. He whimpered softly.

Then, suddenly, the dog's ears perked up. He raised his head, his eyes flashing excitedly.

I heard a sharp growl behind me. From the door.

"Hey—!" I spun around as the door swung open.

And a growling, snarling creature burst in.

Luka!

His eyes moved hungrily from me to Marissa. A pleased grin spread over his wild face.

"No!" Marissa shrieked, backing away from him.

Luka tossed back his long hair with a shake of his head. He opened his mouth in a long howl.

He leapt into the centre of the room. Tossed back his head in a roar. And hurtled towards us.

"Luka—stop!" I begged. "Don't hurt us!"

Luka's grin faded. He lowered his arms. He narrowed his dark eyes at me.

"I'm not going to hurt you," he said softly.

Marissa and I stared back at him in shock. "You—you can talk?" I stammered.

He nodded. "Yes. I can talk. And the first thing I want to say is, congratulations!" His smile returned.

He stepped across the room, walking upright like a human. He shook hands with Marissa, then with me. "Congratulations to both of you," Luka said warmly. "You passed the test."

"But—but—" I could only sputter.

Luka peeled a long strip of fur off his arm. Then he pulled the fur from around his neck. "I'm happy to get this stuff off," he said, peeling more fur from his arm. "It's so hot and itchy—especially when you're running around like a wild man in the forest."

"I'm very confused," I confessed.

Marissa nodded agreement. "Ivanna isn't real," she murmured. She motioned to Ivanna, slumped over the table behind us.

Luka shook his head. "No, she isn't. I built her myself. Just as I built all the creatures you found in my Fantasy Forest."

"But—why?" I choked out. "Why did you build all that?"

"As a test," Luka replied simply. He stepped up behind Ivanna and pulled her up into a sitting position. He brushed the dummy's hair behind her head with his hand. Then he propped the helmet back on her head.

"So many people come to the forest," Luka continued, turning back to Marissa and me. "They come searching for all kinds of treasures. Just as you two have.

"My family has lived in this forest for hundreds of years," Luka explained. "It became our job to protect many of the treasures. And so we built a test forest, to keep out those who were unworthy. To stop the people who don't deserve the wonderful treasures."

"You built the entire forest?" Marissa asked him.

He shook his head. "Just the part that isn't real."

"And how did we pass the test?" I demanded.

"By discovering what was real and what

223

wasn't," Luka replied. "By surviving and triumphing over the unreal."

Marissa stared hard at Ivanna. The dummy's green eyes gazed dully back. "Why did you build Ivanna?" Marissa asked.

Luka grinned proudly. "She is my best creation. She keeps everyone from guessing that I am in charge here. No one believes that a wild wolf man runs the Fantasy Forest. It makes it so easy for me to watch everyone and see how they do on my test."

It all seemed very mysterious to me. But I was too happy it was all over to argue with him.

"And now I shall give you the treasure you came for," Luka announced. He turned quickly and disappeared into the back.

Marissa and I exchanged glances. "I can't believe it!" I whispered. "He's giving us the silver chest containing the Lost Legend! Dad is going to be so amazed!"

"We're going to be rich and famous!" Marissa exclaimed. "And Dad won't be able to tell us we're not helpful—ever again!"

A few seconds later, Luka returned carrying a small silver chest. "Congratulations again," he said solemnly. "I am happy to award you the ancient treasure that you came here to seek. And I wish you good fortune with it."

He placed the silver chest in my hands. It felt

lighter than I expected. The silver gleamed in the light from the candle on the table.

My heart pounded. My hands trembled.

I suddenly felt so excited, I nearly dropped the silver chest! To think that I held the Lost Legend in my hands!

"Thank you," I managed to choke out.

"Yes, thank you," Marissa said. "Now how do we get back to our dad?"

Luka snapped his fingers. Back at the wall, Silverdog leapt to his feet.

"Silverdog will lead you back to your camp," Luka announced. "Stay close behind him, and he will protect you."

"Uh . . . protect us?" I asked, gripping the chest tightly.

Luka nodded. "There are many thieves in the forest. Some of them are real, and some of them are not real. But they all would steal your treasure and make it their own."

"We'll stay close to Silverdog," I promised.

We thanked Luka again. Then we followed the big white dog out of the cabin and back into the forest.

The afternoon sun had started to lower itself behind the trees. It cast an orange glow over the forest floor. The air had already begun to carry an evening chill.

Trotting steadily, the big dog kept his furry tail up high as he led the way, like a flag for us to follow. I carried the chest carefully between my hands and kept my eyes on the dog. Marissa followed close behind.

We walked along a curving path through a patch of tall yellow weeds. Then we made our way around a high clump of evergreen bushes.

On the other side of the bushes, Silverdog led us on to a leaf-covered path. Our boots crunched over the path as we hurried to keep up with the trotting dog.

I gripped the silver chest tightly. I couldn't wait to pull open the lid and gaze at the Lost Legend. To take it out and start to read it.

What was the legend about?

Who wrote it? And when was it written?

So many questions. And I knew they would all be answered as soon as we opened the chest and removed the legend from its hiding-place of five hundred years.

The sun lowered itself behind the trees. Our shadows grew longer. The leaves crunched underfoot.

"Oh—wait!" I cried out when I heard leaves crunching behind us. "Wait—!"

Silverdog trotted on ahead of us.

But Marissa and I stopped.

And listened.

Listened to the crunching footsteps creeping

up fast from the trees behind us.

I felt a chill of fear sweep down my back. "Marissa—we're being followed," I whispered.

"Luka warned us about thieves," Marissa whispered.

The crunching footsteps came closer. I tucked the silver chest under one arm as if protecting a football. My throat tightened. I could barely breathe.

I turned and saw Silverdog trotting on up ahead, his tail still raised behind him. The dog disappeared behind a clump of tall weeds.

"We can't just stand here," Marissa whispered.

The footsteps were approaching faster now. Any moment, I knew, some thief—or *several* thieves—would burst out of the trees and grab the chest away from us.

I turned to the tall weeds. I couldn't see the dog at all now.

"We have to run," Marissa whispered.

I listened to the crunching footsteps.

"We can't outrun him," I told her. "I can't run

very fast. I have to be careful with this chest."

Marissa's blue eyes grew wide with panic. Then her expression changed. "I have an idea, Justin. Let's duck into those trees." She pointed. "The thief will run right past us. Then we'll hide there till he's out of sight."

Was it a good idea?

A terrible idea?

We had no time to think about it. We had to *move*.

We both spun around and started to run to the trees. *Towards* the approaching footsteps.

Would we make it to safety? Could we hide in the trees *before* he came rushing out at us?

I never found out.

About halfway across the grass, I tripped over a fallen branch.

"Ohhh!" I cried out.

And stumbled forward.

The silver chest flew from my hands.

"Noooooo!"

I desperately grabbed for it.

Missed.

Fell hard to my knees.

I watched the chest sail into the air.

And I stared in shock as a big man lumbered out of the dark shadows of the trees, raised his arms, and caught the chest easily.

I stared at the silver chest. Watched the man's hands pull it in, then hold it tightly.

Our chest.

Our Lost Legend.

We had gone through so many horrors to get it. And now someone else had taken it away.

I stared at the chest gripped so tightly in the man's hands. Then I raised my eyes to the man's bearded face.

"Dad!" I cried.

"Dad!" Marissa echoed. "I don't *believe* it!"

Beneath the beard, a grin spread quickly over Dad's face. "I don't believe it, either!" he cried. "Where have you been? Why did you run away? I've been searching the forest for you! Where were you?"

"It's kind of a long story," Marissa told him, rushing forward.

"Yes. Marissa and I have a legend of our own," I said.

Dad set the chest on the ground, and we both hugged him. Dad was so glad to see us, he had tears in his eyes. When we'd finished hugging, he hugged us both again.

"I can't believe I've finally found you!" he exclaimed happily.

"And look what *we've* found!" I declared, pointing to the chest.

Dad's mouth dropped open. When he jumped out and caught the chest, I don't think he realized what he had caught.

"It's—a silver chest!" he exclaimed.

"It's *the* silver chest!" I told him. "The silver chest we came to Brovania to find!"

"But—but—how?"

I'd never seen Dad so confused. Or so excited.

"The Legend of the Lost Legend," he murmured. He carefully lifted the chest off the ground. "This is the most thrilling moment of my life," he said. "How did you *do* this? How did you find this ancient chest? How did you—?"

His voice cracked. I think he was too excited to speak.

"I told you, Dad. It's a very long story," I said.

"At least you can't say we weren't helpful!" Marissa chimed in.

All three of us laughed.

"Do you realize what this will mean to us?" Dad asked, lowering his voice to a whisper. "Do you realize what a thrilling discovery this is?"

He dropped down to his knees to admire the chest. He tenderly ran his hands over the smooth silver of the lid.

"Beautiful. Beautiful," he repeated, grinning.

"Can we open it?" Marissa asked, dropping down on the ground beside him. "Please, Dad? Can we open it and see the Lost Legend?"

"We *have* to see it!" I exclaimed eagerly. "We *have* to!"

Dad nodded. "Yes. We *have* to!" He laughed. "Believe me, I'm even more impatient to see it than you two are!"

He bent over the chest. I saw his hands tremble as he lowered them to the silver clasp.

"Beautiful. Beautiful," he murmured again.

His hands closed around the clasp. He turned it, then gave a sharp tug.

Slowly, slowly, he pulled open the lid.

And all three of us leaned close and gazed into the chest.

We leaned so close over the chest, our heads touched.

"I—I don't *believe* it!" I gasped.

"What *is* it?" Marissa shrieked.

Dad's mouth dropped open. He narrowed his eyes and gazed into the chest. He didn't say a word.

"It—it's an *egg*!" I finally stammered.

The three of us were staring down at a large yellow egg with brown speckles.

"But—where is the Lost Legend?" Marissa demanded. "This can't be it!"

Dad sighed and shook his head. "This isn't the right silver chest," he said softly.

He reached inside and carefully lifted the egg. Then he felt around on the bottom of the chest with his free hand. "Nothing else in here. Just an egg."

He examined the egg, rolling it slowly

between his hands. Then he carefully lowered it back into the chest. "Just an egg," he repeated sadly.

I let out a hoarse cry. "But Marissa and I passed the test!" I wailed. "Luka said he would give us what we came here for!"

"Who is Luka?" Dad asked. He carefully closed the clasp on the chest. Then, with a groan, he climbed to his feet. "Where can we find him?"

Before I could answer, I heard a rustling sound across the clearing. I turned to see Silverdog come trotting out of the weeds.

"Silverdog!" I cried. I rushed forward and petted the dog's big head and the fur around his neck. "Take us back to Luka!" I ordered him. "Luka! Take us to Luka!"

Silverdog wagged his tail. Did that mean he understood?

"Luka!" I repeated. "Take us to Luka!"

Still wagging his bushy tail, the big dog headed past us to the trees. Dad picked up the silver chest. And the three of us followed the dog back through the forest.

Marissa and I hadn't travelled far from the little cabin. A few minutes later, it came into view. Luka hurried out, his face twisted in surprise.

"I didn't expect to see you back here," he said, shaking out his long, dark hair. "Did you get lost?"

234

"No. Not exactly," Marissa replied.

"This is our dad," I told Luka. "We finally found him."

Dad and Luka shook hands.

"Well, why did you come back here?" Luka demanded. He lowered his gaze to the silver chest in Dad's hands. "I gave you what you came here for."

"Not exactly," Dad replied. "It's an egg."

"Yes, I know," Luka said, scratching his jaw.

"But we didn't come here for an egg!" I protested.

Luka narrowed his eyes at us. "You didn't come to the forest in search of the Eternal Egg of Truth?"

"No way," I replied. "Dad brought us here to find the Legend of the Lost Legend."

"Oops!" Luka blushed. "I made a little goof." He looked very upset.

"That's okay," Dad said softly. "Everyone makes mistakes."

Luka shook his head. "I'm so sorry. I usually get it right. I really thought you were searching for the Eternal Egg of Truth."

Still shaking his head, he took the silver chest from Dad's hands. He carried it into the cabin. A few seconds later, he returned. "A thousand apologies," he said.

"But can you help us find the Lost Legend?" I demanded. "Do you have it?"

"Do I have it?" The question seemed to surprise Luka. "No. I don't have it. I think it will be very hard to get it."

"Why?" Dad asked eagerly. "Do you know where it is?"

Luka nodded. "Yes. I can direct you to the people who have the Lost Legend. But I do not think they will part with it. They have been wandering the forest with it for five hundred years. I do not think they will want to give it to you—for any price."

"I—I just want to talk with them!" Dad cried excitedly. "I just want to *see* it with my own eyes!"

"Go in this direction," Luka instructed us, pointing. "Cross two streams, and you will probably find them on a wide, stone clearing. They wander the forest. They never stay in the same place for long. But I think you will find them in the stone clearing if you hurry."

"Thank you!" Dad cried, shaking Luka's hand.

We all thanked Luka. Then we hurried off in the direction he had pointed. We were so excited, all three of us talked at the same time.

"Do you think they'll be friendly?"

"Do you think they'll let us see the Lost Legend?"

"Do you think they'll let me borrow it?" Dad asked. "If I could only borrow it for a few weeks . . ."

"Luka said they might not be friendly."

"He said they might not part with it—for any price."

The journey across the two streams was not difficult. We walked for only an hour.

We were still talking excitedly as we drew near their camp. We stopped on a low hill overlooking a wide patch of stony ground.

The stone clearing.

We could see rows of small tents made of animal hides. Several people, dressed in brown robes, worked to build a fire in the centre of the clearing. A bunch of scrawny grey dogs wrestled and snapped at each other at the edge of the clearing.

"I can't believe it," Dad exclaimed, his eyes searching the small tent village. "I can't believe these wanderers actually *have* the Lost Legend."

"But will they let us *see* it?" I asked.

"Only one way to find out," Dad replied. He led the way down the hill. "Hello, there!" he called out to the wanderers. "Hello!"

"Hello, there! Hello!"

As we stepped on to the stone ground, the scrawny grey dogs stopped wrestling. Barking furiously, they came scurrying up to greet us. They lowered their heads, bared their jagged teeth, and growled.

Marissa, Dad and I stopped. I saw three men in brown robes come running out of tents. They quickly shooed the dogs away. The men, I saw, were as scrawny as the dogs.

"Hello," Dad greeted them warmly. "I am Professor Richard Clarke, and this is Justin and Marissa."

The three men nodded solemnly. But they did not speak.

Two of them were bald. One had long, wavy white hair and a bushy white moustache.

Marissa and I exchanged glances.

I could see that she was as frightened as I

was. These brown-robed wanderers did *not* look friendly.

The white-haired man spoke first. "How did you find us?" he demanded coldly.

"Someone directed us to you," Dad replied.

"Why have you come here, Professor Clarke?" the wanderer asked.

"We're searching for the Legend of the Lost Legend," Dad told him.

The three men all gasped in shock. They leaned close and whispered furiously to each other.

When they'd finished their excited conversation, they turned back to us. But they didn't speak.

"Do you have it?" Dad asked eagerly. "Do you have the Lost Legend?"

"Yes," the white-haired man replied. "Yes, we have it."

He whispered something to the two bald men. They spun around, their long robes twirling with them, and hurried away.

A few seconds later, they returned. One of them carried a small silver chest.

"Oh, my goodness!" Dad declared, his eyes bulging. "Is that it? Is that really it? Is that the Lost Legend?"

"Yes," the white-haired man replied. "Do you want it?"

"Huh?" all three of us cried.

The wanderer shoved the chest into my hands. I was so shocked, I nearly dropped it!

"It is yours," the white-haired man said. He stepped back.

Dad swallowed hard. "Are you *sure*?" he cried. "Are you sure you want to give it to us?"

"Yes. Take it," the man replied quickly. "Goodbye."

He and the other two turned and walked quickly back to their tents. To our surprise, they instantly began to pack up.

Dozens of wanderers began pulling up tents, packing up supplies, putting out the campfire. In minutes, they had scurried away.

The stone clearing stood bare. No sign they had ever been there.

"How strange," Dad said. "How totally strange."

We began to walk away from the clearing. I think all three of us were in shock or something. I know I was completely stunned.

"They handed the treasure over to us without a word," Dad said, rubbing his beard. "Why did they *do* that? Why did they give this treasure to us without asking for anything in return? I just can't believe it."

I still had the chest in my arms. After we had walked for a short while, I stopped. "Where are we going?" I demanded. "Let's open the chest. Let's take a look at it!"

"Yes!" Dad agreed. "I am so surprised—so stunned—I guess I don't know what I'm doing!"

He took the chest from me and carefully set it down on the ground. "Let's see it. Let's finally see it!"

Carefully, he unlatched the lid and opened the chest. Then he reached inside—and pulled out a manuscript. A thick stack of yellowed paper with tiny black writing all over it.

"Yes!" Dad whispered happily. "Yes!"

He gripped the ancient legend tightly in both hands and held it down so that Marissa and I could see it.

"Wow!" Marissa cried. "It really looks five hundred years old—doesn't it?"

"Dad, what does it say on the top page?" I asked, struggling to make out the words.

"Uh . . . let's see," Dad replied. He raised the manuscript close to his face, squinted hard at the tiny words, and then read them out loud:

"WHOEVER OWNS THE LOST LEGEND WILL BE LOST FOR EVER."

"Huh? What does *that* mean?" I cried.

Dad shrugged. "It doesn't really mean anything. It's just part of the legend."

"Are you sure?" Marissa demanded in a trembling voice.

Dad stared down at the manuscript. "'Lost for ever . . .'" he murmured. "*Whoever owns the Lost Legend will be lost for ever.*'"

Then he raised his eyes to the trees that surrounded us. "Hey—where are we?"

All three of us gazed around at the strange, dark trees.

We had wandered away from the stone clearing. Now nothing looked familiar.

"Where are we?" Dad repeated.

"We . . . we're lost," I whispered.

Goosebumps

Attack of the
Jack-O'-Lanterns

"Where are you going, Elf?" Dad called from the study.

"Don't call me Elf!" I shouted back. "My name is Drew."

Dad thinks it's really cute to call me Elf, but I hate it. He calls me Elf because I'm tiny for a twelve-year-old. And I have short, straight black hair and sort of a pointy chin and a pointy little nose.

If you looked like an elf, would you want people calling you Elf?

Of course not.

One day my best friend, Walker Parkes, heard my dad call me Elf. So Walker tried it. "What's up, Elf?" Walker said.

I stamped on Walker's foot as hard as I could, and he never called me that again.

"Where are you going, *Drew*?" Dad called from the study.

"Out," I told him, and slammed the front door

behind me. I like to keep my parents guessing. I try never to give them a straight answer.

You might say I'm as mischievous as an elf. But if you said it, I'd stamp on *your* foot, too!

I'm tough. Ask anyone. They'll tell you that Drew Brockman is tough. When you're the shrimpiest girl in your class, you've *got* to be tough.

Actually, I wasn't going anywhere. I was waiting for my friends to come to my house. I walked down to the street to look out for them.

I took a deep breath. The people in the corner house had a fire going in their fireplace. The white smoke floated out from their chimney. It smelled so sweet and piney.

I love autumn. It means Hallowe'en is on the way.

Hallowe'en is my favourite holiday. I suppose I like it so much because it gives me a chance to look like someone else. Or some*thing* else.

It's the one night of the year that I don't have to look like pointy-chinned me.

But I have a problem with Hallowe'en. Two kids in my class are the problem. Tabitha Weiss and Lee Winston.

For the past two years, Tabby and Lee have totally *ruined* Hallowe'en for Walker and me.

I'm so angry about it. Walker is angry, too. Our favourite holiday *ruined* because of two stuck-up kids who think they can do whatever they want.

Grrrrrrrr.

Just thinking about it makes me want to punch someone!

My other friends, Shane and Shana Martin, are upset about it, too. Shane and Shana are brother and sister, twins my age. They live in the house next door, and we hang out a lot.

Shane and Shana don't look like anyone else I know. They both have very round faces with curly ringlets of blond hair. They have red cheeks and cheery smiles, and they're both short and quite chunky.

My dad says they're roly-poly. Dad always thinks of something horrible to say about *everyone*!

Anyway, the twins are as angry as Walker and me about Tabby and Lee. And *this* Hallowe'en, we're going to do something about it.

Only we don't know what we're going to do.

That's why they're coming over to my house to discuss it.

How did the Tabby and Lee problem start? Well, I have to go back two years to explain it to you.

I remember it so clearly.

Walker and I were ten. We were just hanging out in front of my house. Walker had his bike on its side and was doing something to the spokes on one wheel.

It was a beautiful autumn day. Down the block, someone was burning a big pile of leaves. It's against the law here in Riverdale. My dad always threatens to call the police when someone burns leaves. But I love the smell.

Walker was fiddling with his bike, and I was watching him. I forget what we were talking about. I glanced up—and there stood Tabby and Lee.

Tabby looked as perfect as always. "Little Miss Perfect." That's what Dad calls her—and for once, he's right.

The wind was blowing pretty hard. But her long, straight blonde hair stayed in place. It didn't fly out all over her head like mine did.

Tabby has perfect creamy-white skin and perfectly green eyes that sparkle a lot. She's very pretty, and she knows it.

Sometimes it takes all my strength not to shake both hands in her hair and mess it all up!

Lee is tall and good-looking, with dark brown eyes and a great, warm smile. Lee is African-American, and he sort of struts when he walks and acts real cool, like the rappers on MTV videos.

The girls at school all think he's terrific. But I can never understand a word he says. That's because he always has a huge wad of green-apple bubble gum in his mouth.

"Mmmmmbbb mmmmbbbbb." Lee stared down at Walker's bike and mumbled something.

"Hey," I said. "What's up, guys?"

Tabby made a disgusted face and pointed a finger at me. "Drew, you have something hanging from your nose," she said.

"Oh—!" I shot my hand up and rubbed the bottom of my nose. Nothing there.

"Sorry," Tabby sniggered. "It only looked like you did."

Tabby and Lee both laughed.

Tabby is always playing mean jokes like that on me. She knows I'm self-conscious about my looks. So I always fall for her stupid tricks.

"Nice bike," Lee mumbled to Walker. "How many speeds?"

"It's a twelve-speed," Walker told him.

Lee sneered. "Mine is a forty-two-speed."

"Huh?" Walker jumped to his feet. "There's no such thing as a forty-two-speed!" he cried.

"Mine is," Lee insisted, still sneering. "It's specially made."

He blew a big green bubble-gum bubble. That's hard to do while you're sneering.

I wanted to pop it all over his smug face. But he stepped back and popped it himself.

"Have you had a haircut?" Tabby asked me, studying my windblown hair.

"No," I replied.

"I didn't think so," she said. She smoothed her perfect hair back with one hand.

"Grrrrrrr." I couldn't help it. I balled my hands into fists and let out an angry growl.

I growl a lot. Sometimes I don't even know I'm doing it.

"Mummmmmbb mmmmbbbbb." Lee said something. Bubble-gum juice ran down his chin.

"Excuse me?" I asked.

"I'm having a Hallowe'en party," he repeated.

My heart started to pound. "A real Hallowe'en party?" I demanded. "With everyone in costumes, and hot apple cider, and games and bobbing for apples and scary stories?"

Lee nodded. "Yes. A real Hallowe'en party. At my house on Hallowe'en night. You guys want to come?"

"Sure!" Walker and I replied.

Big mistake. *Really* big mistake.

The Hallowe'en party was already crowded with kids from school when Walker and I showed up. Lee's parents had orange and black streamers strung up all over the living room. Three huge jack-o'-lanterns grinned at us from the window seat by the front window.

Of course Tabby was the first person I ran into. Even in costume, she wasn't hard to recognize. She was dressed as a princess.

Perfect?

She wore a frilly pink princess-type gown with long, puffy sleeves and a high, lacy collar. And she had her blonde hair pinned up with a sparkly rhinestone tiara in it.

She smiled her lipsticked lips at me. "Is that you, Drew?" she asked, pretending she didn't recognize me. "What are you supposed to be? A mouse?"

"No!" I protested. "I'm not a mouse. I'm a Klingon. Don't you ever watch *Star Trek*?"

Tabby sniggered. "Are you *sure* you're not a mouse?"

She turned and walked away. She had a pleased smile on her face. She gets such a thrill from insulting me.

I growled under my breath and searched for someone else to talk to. I found Shane and Shana in front of the fireplace. The twins were easy to recognize. They were both big, puffy white snowmen.

"Excellent costumes!" I greeted them.

They wore two white snowballs. One big snowball over their bodies. A smaller snowball over their heads.

The snowman faces had eyeholes cut in them. But I couldn't tell Shane from Shana. "What is the snow made of?" I asked.

"Polystyrene," Shana answered. She has a high, squeaky voice. So now I knew who was who. "We carved them out of big blocks of it."

"Cool," I said.

"Great party, huh?" Shane chimed in. "Everyone from our class is here. Did you see Bryna Morse's costume? She sprayed her whole body with silver spray paint. Her face and hair, too!"

"What's she supposed to be?" I demanded, searching the crowded room for her. "Silver Surfer?"

"No. I think the Statue of Liberty," Shane replied. "She was carrying a plastic torch."

A loud crackle in the fireplace made me jump. Most of the lights were off, giving the room a dark, Hallowe'en mood. The fire made long shadows dance over the floor.

I turned and saw Walker making his way towards us. His entire body was wrapped in bandages and gauze. He was a mummy.

"I'm in trouble," he announced.

"What's your problem?" Shane asked.

"My mum did a terrible wrapping job," Walker complained. "I'm coming unravelled." He struggled to retie the loose bandages around his neck.

"Aaaagh!" He let out an angry cry. "The whole thing is coming undone!"

"Are you wearing clothes underneath?" Shana asked.

Shane and I laughed. I pictured Walker huddled in the middle of the party in his underwear, piles of bandages at his feet.

"Yes. I've got my clothes on underneath the costume," Walker replied. "But if these bandages all come undone, I'll fall on my face!"

"Hey—what's up?" Lee interrupted. He wore a Batman costume, but I recognized his dark eyes under the mask. And I recognized his voice.

"Awesome party," Shana said.

"Yeah. Awesome," I repeated.

Lee started to reply. But a thunderous *crash* made everyone gasp.

We all froze. "What was *that*?" Lee cried.

The crowded room grew silent.

I heard another crash. Bumping sounds. Low voices.

"It—it's coming from the basement!" Lee stammered. He pulled off the Batman mask. His bushy hair fell over his face, but I could see his frightened expression.

We all turned to the open doorway at the far end of the living room. Beyond the doorway, stairs led down to Lee's basement.

"Oh—!" Lee gasped as we heard another crash.

Then heavy footsteps—up the basement stairs.

"Someone is in the house!" Lee shrieked in terror. "Someone has broken in!"

"Mum! Dad!" Lee cried. His voice rang out shrilly in the silent living room. The rest of us had all frozen in place.

A shiver ran down my back as I listened to the heavy footsteps treading up the stairs.

"Mum! Dad! Help!" Lee called again, his eyes bulging with fear.

No reply.

He took off towards their bedroom at the back of the house. "Mum? Dad?"

I started to run after him. But he returned to the living room a few seconds later, his whole body trembling. "My parents—they've *gone*!"

"Call the police!" someone shouted.

"Yes! Call nine-one-one!" Walker screamed.

Lee hurtled to the phone beside the couch. His foot kicked over a can of Pepsi on the rug. But he didn't notice.

He grabbed the phone receiver and jammed it to his ear. I saw him push the emergency number. But then he turned to us and let the phone fall from his hand. "It's dead. The line is dead!"

Some kids gasped. A few cried out.

I turned to Walker and opened my mouth to speak. But before I could get a sound out, two bulky figures burst out from the basement doorway.

"Noooooo—!" Lee let out a horrified howl. Tabby stepped up and huddled close beside him. Her heavily made-up eyes were wide with fright. She grabbed Lee's arm.

The two intruders moved quickly into the living-room entrance and blocked the doorway. One of them had a blue wool ski mask pulled down over his face. The other wore a rubber gorilla mask.

They both wore black leather jackets over black jeans.

"Party time!" the gorilla shouted in a gruff voice. He laughed. A cruel laugh. "Party time, everyone!"

Several kids cried out. My heart started to pound in my chest. I suddenly felt hot and cold at the same time.

"Who are you?" Lee demanded over the frightened cries of some kids. "How did you get in? Where are my parents?"

"Parents?" the guy in the ski mask replied. He had bright blue eyes, almost as blue as the wool mask that covered his face. "Do you have parents?"

They both laughed.

"Where are they?" Lee cried.

"I think they ran away when they saw us coming!" the guy said through the ski mask.

Lee swallowed hard. A tiny gulping sound escaped his throat.

Tabby stepped in front of him. "You can't come in here!" she shouted angrily to the two intruders. "We're having a party!"

The gorilla turned to his partner and laughed. They both laughed loudly, tossing back their heads.

"It's *our* party now!" the gorilla announced. "We're taking over!"

Hushed gasps rang out around the room. My legs suddenly felt rubbery and weak. I grabbed Walker's shoulder to keep from collapsing.

"Wh-what are you going to do?" Tabby demanded.

"Everybody down on the floor!" the guy in the ski mask ordered.

"You can't do this!" Tabby screamed.

"We're just kids!" someone else cried. "Are you going to rob us? We don't have any money!"

I saw Shane and Shana huddled together by the fireplace. Their faces were hidden by their snowman costumes. But I knew they must be terrified, too.

"*Down on the floor!*" both intruders screamed.

The room echoed with heavy thuds and the rustle of costumes as we all obediently dropped to the floor.

"You, too!" the gorilla screamed at Shane and Shana.

"It's impossible! How can we get down in these big snowballs?" Shana cried.

"Get down on the floor anyway," the gorilla ordered nastily.

"Get down—or we'll push you down," the ski-masked guy threatened.

I watched Shane and Shana struggle to lower themselves to the floor. They had to pull off their bottom snowballs to get on to their knees. Shana's snowball broke in half as she worked to pull it off.

"Okay—press-ups, everybody!" the gorilla ordered.

"Huh?" Confused cries rose up through the room.

"Press-ups!" the gorilla repeated. "You all know how to do press-ups—right?"

"How—how many do we have to do?" Walker asked. He knelt close beside me on the rug in front of the coffee table.

"Do them for a couple of hours," the ski-masked guy replied.

"Hours?" several kids cried out.

"A few hours of press-ups will get you all warmed up," the gorilla said. "Then we'll think of something harder for you to do!"

"Yeah. *Much* harder!" his partner added. Then they both burst out laughing again.

"You can't do this!" I screamed. My voice came out high and tiny, like a mouse voice.

Other kids protested, too. I turned to the door. The guy in the ski mask had moved into the living room. But the gorilla was still blocking any escape.

"*Get started!*" the gorilla ordered.

"Or we'll make it *three* hours!" his partner added.

I heard a lot of groans and complaints. But we all dropped on to our stomachs and started doing press-ups.

What choice did we have?

"We can't do this for two hours!" Walker protested breathlessly. "We'll *faint!*"

He raised and dropped, raised and dropped, close beside me on the floor. His mummy costume was unravelling with each move he made.

"Faster!" the gorilla ordered. "Come on. Speed it up!"

I had done only four or five press-ups, and my arms already started to ache. I don't get much exercise, except for bike riding and swimming in the summer.

There was no way I'd last for more than ten or fifteen minutes.

I raised my eyes to the front of the room— and saw a sight that made me cry out in shock.

"Walker—look!" I whispered.

"Hunnh?" he groaned.

I poked Walker in the side.

He lost his balance and hit the floor. "Hey, Drew—! What's your problem?" he groaned.

We both turned our eyes to the doorway.

And saw to our surprise that Tabby and Lee weren't down on the floor with the rest of us. They had joined the two intruders in front of the doorway.

And they both had wide, gleeful grins on their faces.

I stopped the press-ups and raised myself to my knees. I saw Lee start to laugh.

Tabby joined him. She laughed so hard, her tiara shook. They slapped each other a high five.

All around me on the floor, some kids were still working away, pushing themselves up, then down, up, then down. Groaning and grunting as they obediently did their press-ups.

But Walker and I had stopped. We were both on our knees, watching Tabby and Lee. The two creeps were laughing and celebrating.

I was about to cry out in anger—when the two intruders tugged off their masks.

I instantly recognized the boy with the gorilla mask. He was Todd Jeffrey, a high-school kid who lives next door to Lee.

I knew the ski-mask kid, too. His name was Joe Something-or-other. He is a friend of Todd's.

Todd brushed his coppery hair back off his forehead. His hair was wet, his face was red, and he was sweating. I suppose it was hot inside that rubber mask.

Joe tossed his ski mask to the floor. He shook his head, laughing at us. "All a joke, guys!" he called out. "Happy Hallowe'en!"

All the other kids had stopped the press-ups. But no one had moved from the floor. I think we were too shocked to stand up.

"Just a party joke!" Lee chimed in, grinning.

"Did we scare you?" Tabby asked coyly.

"Grrrrrr!" I let out the loudest growl I've ever growled. I wanted to leap up, grab the tiara off Princess Tabby's head, and wrap it around her neck!

Todd and Joe slapped each other a high five. They picked up cans of Pepsi and tilted them up over their mouths.

"You can get up now!" Lee announced, sniggering.

"Wow! You guys looked so *scared*!" Tabby cried gleefully. "I think we really fooled you!"

"I don't believe this," Walker muttered, shaking his head. The wrapping had fallen from his face. Bandages drooped loosely over his shoulders. "I really don't believe this. What a mean, rotten joke."

I climbed up shakily and helped Walker to his feet. I heard Shane and Shana grumbling behind us. Their costumes were totally wrecked.

Kids were grumbling and complaining. Tabby and Lee were the only ones laughing. No one else thought the joke was the least bit funny.

I started across the room to tell the two creeps what I thought of their stupid joke. But Lee's parents burst into the room, pulling off their coats.

"We went next door to the Jeffreys'," Lee's mum announced. Then she saw Todd. "Oh, hi, Todd. We were just at your house, visiting your parents. What are you doing over here? Helping Lee out with the party?"

"Kind of," Todd replied, grinning.

"How's the party going?" Lee's dad asked.

"Great," Lee told him. "Just great, Dad."

And that's how Tabby and Lee ruined Hallowe'en two years ago.

Walker and I—and Shane and Shana, too—were all really upset.

No. We were more than upset. We were furious.

Hallowe'en is our favourite holiday. And we don't like to see it ruined because of a nasty practical joke.

So, last year we decided to get even.

"We need special decorations," Shana said. "Not the same old pumpkins and skeletons."

"Yeah. Something scarier," Shane chimed in.

"I think jack-o'-lanterns can be really scary," I insisted. "Especially when you put candles in them. And their dark faces light up with those jagged, evil grins."

"Jack-o'-lanterns are babyish," Walker argued. "No one is afraid of a jack-o'-lantern. Shana is right. If we're going to scare Tabby and Lee, we need something better."

It was a week before Hallowe'en. The four of us were hard at work at my house. We were working on *my* Hallowe'en party.

Yes. Last year, the party was at my house.

Why did I decide to have the party? For only one reason.

For revenge.

For revenge on Tabby and Lee.

Walker, Shane, Shana and I had spent the

whole year talking about it, dreaming up plans. Dreaming up the most frightening scares we could imagine.

We didn't want to pull a nasty joke like having people break into the house.

That was *too* nasty. And too frightening.

Some of my friends *still* have bad dreams about guys in ski masks and gorilla masks.

The four of us didn't want to terrify *all* of our guests. We just wanted to embarrass Tabby and Lee—and scare them out of their skins!

Now, a week before the big night, we were sitting around my living room after dinner. We should have been doing homework. But Hallowe'en was too near.

We had no time for homework. We had to spend all of our time making evil plans.

Shane and Shana had a lot of really frightening ideas. They both look so sweet and innocent. But once you get to know them, they're pretty weird.

Walker and I wanted to keep our scares simple. The simpler, the scarier. That's what we thought.

I wanted to drop fake cobwebs over Tabby and Lee from the stairway. I know a shop that sells really sticky, scratchy cobwebs.

Walker has a tarantula that he keeps in a glass cage in his room. A live tarantula. He thought maybe we could tangle the tarantula in the cobwebs and then drop it in Tabby's hair.

Not a bad idea.

Walker also wanted to cut a trapdoor in the living-room floor. When Tabby and Lee stepped on the spot, we'd open the trapdoor, and they would disappear into the basement.

I had to reject that idea. I liked it. But I wasn't sure how Mum and Dad would react when they discovered us sawing up the floor.

Also, I just wanted to terrify the two creeps. I didn't want to break their necks.

"Where are we going to put the fake blood puddles?" Shane asked.

He held a red plastic puddle of blood in each hand. He and his sister had bought a dozen fake blood puddles at a joke shop. They came in different sizes, and looked very real.

"And don't forget the green slime," Shana reminded us. She had three plastic bags of slime beside her.

Walker and I opened one of the bags and felt the slimy, sticky, oozy gunk. "Where did you buy this?" I asked. "At the same shop?"

"No. It came out of Shana's nose!" Shane joked.

With an angry cry, Shana hoisted up one of the bags. She swung it in front of her, threatening to smack her brother with it.

He laughed and bounced off the couch.

"Whoa! Careful!" I cried. "If that bag breaks—"

"Maybe we can hang the slime from the ceiling," Walker suggested.

"Yeah! Cool!" Shane cried excitedly. "And it could drip down on to Tabby and Lee."

"Maybe we could cover them in it!" Walker added excitedly. "And they'd look like two sticky, green blobs."

"Glub glub glub!" Shana thrashed out her arms and pretended she was drowning under a puddle of slime.

"Will it stick to the ceiling?" I asked. "How will we keep it up there long enough? How will we get the two of them to stand under it?"

I'm the practical one in the group. They have a lot of wild ideas. But they never know how to make them work.

That's my job.

"I'm not sure," Walker replied. He jumped up from his chair. "I'm going to get something to drink."

"What if the slime started to spew out of the jack-o'-lanterns?" Shane suggested. "That would be quite scary—wouldn't it?"

"What if we had fake blood gush out of the jack-o'-lanterns?" Shana said. "That would be even scarier."

"We have to trap Tabby and Lee somehow," Shane suggested, thinking hard. "All this slime

268

and cobwebs and blood is good. But we have to make them think they're really in danger. We have to make them think that something *terrible* is really going to happen to them."

I started to agree—but the lights went out.

"Oh—!" I uttered a cry of surprise, blinking in the sudden darkness. "What's happened?"

Shane and Shana didn't reply.

The curtains were drawn. So no light entered the living room from outside. The room was so dark, I couldn't see my two friends sitting right opposite me!

And then, I heard a dry, whispered voice. A frightening whisper, so close, so close to my ear:

> *"Come with me.*
> *Come home with me now.*
> *Come home to where you belong.*
> *Come home—to the grave."*

Staring into the darkness, the whispered words sent a shiver down my back.

"Come with me.
Come home with me now.
Come home to where you belong.
Come to your grave, Tabby and Lee.
I have come for you and you alone.
Come, Tabby and Lee. Come with me now."

"That's excellent!" I cried.

The lights flashed back on. Opposite me, Shane and Shana clapped and cheered.

"Good job, Walker!" I turned to congratulate him.

He set his portable tape player on the coffee table in front of us and rewound the tape. "I think it will scare them," he said.

"It scared *me*!" I told him. "And I knew what it was."

"When the lights go out and that voice starts to whisper, it will creep *everyone* out!" Shana exclaimed. "Especially with the tape player right under the couch."

"Who recorded the voice?" Shane asked Walker. "Did you do it?"

Walker nodded.

"Cool," Shane said. He turned to me. "But, Drew, I still think you should let Shana and me do some of *our* scares on Tabby and Lee."

"Let's save those for when we really need them," I replied.

I bent down and opened one of the plastic bags. I dug a hand in and pulled out a big chunk of green slime. It felt cold and gooey in my hand.

I worked it around in my palm, squeezing it and shaping it. Then I rolled it into a ball.

"Think it's sticky enough to hang from the ceiling?" I asked. "It would be a nice effect to have it running down the walls. I think—"

"No. I've got a better idea," Walker interrupted. "The lights all go out—right? And the creepy voice starts to whisper. And when it whispers their names—when it whispers, 'Come to your grave, Tabby and Lee'—then someone sneaks up behind each of them and drops a huge glob of slime on their heads."

"That's cool!" Shane declared. We all laughed and cheered.

We had some good ideas. But we needed more.

I didn't want to slip up. I didn't want Tabby and Lee to think it was funny, all a big joke.

I wanted them to be SCARED—with a capital S-C-A-R-E-D.

So we thought of more scary ideas. And more ideas.

We worked all week. From after school until late at night. Setting traps. Hiding little creepy surprises all over the living room.

We carved the ugliest jack-o'-lanterns you've ever seen. And we filled them with real-looking plastic cockroaches.

We made an eight-foot-tall, papier-mâché monster. And we rigged it to fall out of the hall cupboard when we pulled a string.

We bought real-looking rubber snakes and worms and spiders and hid them all around the house.

We didn't eat or sleep. We dragged ourselves through school, thinking only about more ways to terrify our two special guests.

Finally, Hallowe'en arrived.

The four of us gathered at my house. We were too tense to sit still or even stand still. We moved around the house, barely speaking to each other. And we carefully checked and rechecked all of the frightening traps and tricks we had prepared.

I had never worked so hard in all my life. Never!

I spent so much time getting ready for the party—and our revenge—that I didn't even think of my Hallowe'en costume until the very last minute.

And so I ended up wearing the same Klingon costume I had worn the year before.

Walker was a pirate that year. He had a patch over one eye and wore a striped shirt and a parrot on one shoulder.

Shane and Shana had dressed as some kind of blobby creatures. I couldn't really tell *what* they were supposed to be.

We didn't care about our costumes. We only cared about scaring Tabby and Lee.

And then, as we paced the living room nervously, one hour before the party was to start, the phone rang.

And we received a call that filled us all with horror.

I was standing right next to the phone when it rang. The harsh buzz nearly made me jump out of my skin. Was I a little tense? YES!

I grabbed the phone in the middle of the first ring. "Hello?"

I heard a familiar voice on the other end. "Hi, Drew. It's Tabby."

"Tabby!" I cried. I decided she was calling to find out what time the party started. "The party starts at eight," I said. "But if you and Lee—"

"That's why I'm calling," Tabby interrupted. "Lee and I can't come tonight."

"Huh?"

The phone dropped out of my hand. It clattered to the floor.

I dived to pick up the receiver, stumbled, and nearly knocked the whole table over.

"What? What did you say?" I demanded.

"Lee and I can't come." Tabby repeated the chilling words. "We're going to Lee's cousin's

274

instead. His cousin gets to trick-or-treat until midnight. He does four different neighbourhoods. He promised we'll get bag and bags of sweets. Sorry."

"But, Tabby—" I started to protest weakly.

"Sorry," she said. "See you. Bye."

She hung up.

I let out a hoarse wail and sank to my knees on the floor.

"What's wrong?" Walker demanded.

"They—they—they—" I couldn't get the words out.

My three friends huddled around me. Walker tried to pull me to my feet. But my head was spinning. I didn't want to stand up.

"They're *not coming*!" I finally managed to choke out. "Not coming."

"Oh," Walker replied softly. Shane and Shana shook their heads glumly, but didn't say a word.

We all stayed frozen in place, stunned, too miserable to talk. Thinking about all the work . . . all the planning and all the hard work.

A *whole year* of planning and work.

I'm not going to cry, I told myself. I feel like crying, but I'm not going to.

I climbed shakily to my feet. And glanced at the couch.

"What is *that*?" I shrieked.

Everyone turned and saw what I saw. A huge,

ugly hole in one of the brown leather couch cushions.

"Oh no!" Shana wailed. "I was playing with a ball of green slime. I must have dropped it on to the couch when I stood up. It—it *burned a hole* in the cushion!"

"Quick—cover it up before Mum and Dad see—" I started.

Of course Mum and Dad came strolling into the living room. "How's it going?" Dad asked. "All ready for your guests?"

I crossed my fingers and prayed they wouldn't see the huge hole in the couch.

"Good heavens! What happened to the couch?" Mum shrieked.

It took Mum and Dad a long time to get over the ruined couch.

And it took me even longer to get over the ruined party.

That's how it went *last* Hallowe'en. Two years. Two years of ruined Hallowe'ens.

Now it's a year later.

Hallowe'en time again. This year, we have *twice* as much reason to get revenge on Tabby and Lee.

If only we had a plan . . .

"This year I'm a space princess," Tabby announced.

She had her blonde hair piled high once again, with the same rhinestone tiara in it. And she wore the same long, lacy dress.

The same costume as two years ago. But to add the outer-space look, Tabby had painted her face bright green.

She always has to be a princess, I thought bitterly. Green or not green, she's still a princess.

Lee showed up in a cape and tights and said he was Superman. He said it was his little brother's costume. He told us why he didn't have time to get a costume of his own. But I couldn't understand him because of the big wad of bubble gum in his mouth.

Walker and I had decided to be ghosts. We cut eyeholes in bedsheets, and armholes, and that was that.

My sheet dragged behind me on the grass. I should have cut it shorter. But it was too late. We were already on our way to trick-or-treat.

"Where are Shane and Shana?" Lee asked.

"We'll catch up with them," I replied. I raised my trick-or-treat bag in front of me. "Let's get going."

The four of us stepped out into a clear, cold night. A pale half-moon floated low over the houses. The grass shone grey under a light blanket of frost.

We stopped at the bottom of my driveway. An estate car rumbled by. I saw two big dogs peering out the back window. The driver slowed to stare at us as she passed by.

"Where shall we start?" Tabby asked.

Lee mumbled something I didn't understand.

"I want to trick-or-treat all night!" Walker exclaimed. "This may be our last trick-or-treat night ever."

"Excuse me? What do you mean?" Tabby demanded, turning her green face to him.

"Next year, we'll be teenagers," Walker explained. "We'll be too old to trick-or-treat."

Quite a sad thought.

I tried to take a deep breath of cool air. But I had forgotten to cut a nose or mouth in the sheet. We hadn't even left my front garden, and I was already starting to feel hot!

"Let's start at The Willows," I suggested.

The Willows is a neighbourhood of small houses. It starts on the other side of a small wood, just two blocks away.

"Why The Willows?" Tabby demanded, fiddling with her tiara.

"Because the houses are very close together," I told her. "We won't have to walk much, and we'll get a lot of sweets. No long driveways to walk up and down."

"Sounds good," Lee agreed.

We started walking along the kerb. Across the street, I saw two monsters and a skeleton making their way across a front garden. Little kids, followed by a father.

The wind fluttered my costume as we walked. My shoes crunched over frost-covered dead leaves. The sky seemed to grow darker as we made our way past the bare black trees of the woods.

A few minutes later, we reached the first block of The Willows. Street lights cast a warm yellow glow over the neighbourhood. A lot of the houses were decorated with orange and green lights, cut-outs of witches and goblins, and flickering jack-o'-lanterns.

The four of us began walking from house to house, gleefully yelling "Trick or treat!" and collecting all kinds of sweets.

People oohed and aahed over Tabby's princess costume. She was the only one in our group who had bothered to put on a decent costume. So I suppose she stood out.

We passed by a lot of other kids as we made our way down the block. Most of them appeared younger than us. One kid was dressed as a milk carton. He even had all the nutritional information printed on one side.

It took us about half an hour to do both sides of the street. The Willows ended in a cul-de-sac. Kind of a dead end.

"Where to next?" Tabby asked.

"Whoa. Wait. One more house," Walker said. He pointed to a small brick house set back in the trees.

"I didn't see that one," I said. "I suppose because it's the only house that isn't right on the street."

"The lights are on, and they've got a pumpkin in the window," Walker announced. "Let's check it out."

We trooped up to the front doorstep and pushed the doorbell. The front door swung open instantly. A small, white-haired woman poked out her head. She squinted through thick glasses at us.

"Trick or treat!" the four of us chanted.

"Oh my goodness!" she exclaimed. She pressed wrinkled hands against her cheeks. "What wonderful costumes!"

Huh? Wonderful costumes? I thought. Two

bedsheets and a borrowed Superman suit from last year?

The old woman turned back into the house. "Forrest, come and see this!" she called. "You've got to see these costumes."

I heard a man cough from somewhere deep inside the house.

"Come in. Please come in," the old woman pleaded. "I want my husband to see you." She stepped back to make room for us to enter.

The four of us hesitated.

"Come in!" she insisted. "Forrest has to see your costumes. But it's hard for him to get up. Please!"

Tabby led the way into the house. We stepped into a tiny, dimly lit living room. A fire blazed in a small brick fireplace against one wall. The room felt like a blast furnace. It had to be five hundred degrees in there!

The woman shut the front door behind us. "Forrest! Forrest!" she called. She turned to us and smiled. "He's in the back room. Follow me."

She opened the door and let us enter. To my surprise, the back room was enormous.

And jammed with kids in costumes.

"Whoa!" I cried out, startled. My eyes quickly swept the room.

Most of the kids had taken off their masks. Some of them were crying. Some were red-faced and angry. Several kids sat cross-legged on the floor, their expressions glum.

"What's going on?" Tabby demanded shrilly. Her eyes bulged wide with fear.

"What are they all doing here?" Lee asked, swallowing hard.

A red-faced little man with shaggy white hair came hobbling out from the corner, leaning on a white cane. "I like your costumes," he said, grinning at us.

"We—we have to go now," Tabby stammered.

We all turned to the door. The old woman had shut it behind her.

I glanced back at the kids in costumes. There were at least two dozen of them. They all looked so frightened and unhappy.

"We have to go," Tabby repeated shrilly.

"Yeah. Let us out of here," Lee insisted.

The old man smiled. The woman stepped up beside him. "You have to stay," she said. "We like looking at your costumes."

"You can't go," the man added, leaning heavily on his cane. "We have to look at your costumes."

"Huh? What are you *saying*? How long are you going to keep us here?" Tabby cried.

"For ever," the old couple replied in unison.

That was my day-dream.

I was down by the street in front of my house, waiting for my friends to show up. And day-dreaming about Tabby and Lee being trapped by a weird old couple who liked to collect trick-or-treaters and keep them for ever.

Of course, in my day-dream, Walker and I sneaked out a side door.

But Tabby and Lee were caught before they could escape. And they were never seen again.

Nice day-dream, huh?

I was still picturing the whole thing when Walker, Shane and Shana finally arrived. And we eagerly trooped inside and up to my room.

"Drew, why are you grinning like that?" Shana demanded, dropping down on to the edge of my bed.

"I was just having a very funny day-dream," I told her. "About Tabby and Lee."

"What could be funny about those two creeps?" Walker demanded. He picked up a tennis ball from the floor and tossed it to Shane. The two of them started tossing the ball back and forth across my room.

"It was very funny," I replied, sitting up and stretching. "Especially the ending."

I told them the whole day-dream. I could see from the smiles on their faces that they enjoyed it.

But Shana scolded me. "We don't have time for day-dreams, Drew. We need a real plan. It's almost Hallowe'en."

Walker tossed the tennis ball too high. It smashed into my dresser lamp and knocked it over.

Shane hurtled towards the lamp and made a diving catch before it hit the floor.

"Way to go!" Walker cried. "Catch of the Month!" He slapped Shane a high five. He hit Shane so hard, the poor guy almost dropped the lamp.

"Grrrrrrr!" I growled at Walker and pointed to the desk chair. "Sit down. We have serious thinking to do."

"She's right," Shana agreed. "We have to scare Tabby and Lee out of their skins this year. We have to pay them back for the last two years. We *have* to!"

"So what are we going to do?" Walker

demanded, dropping his long, lanky body into the desk chair. "Hide behind some bushes and yell 'Boo!'?"

Bad attitude.

"I've been thinking of some really scary things we could do at a party," I started. "I think—"

"No party!" Shana interrupted.

"Right. No party," her twin agreed. "We worked so hard on last year's party. And then Tabby and Lee didn't show up."

"Grrrrr." Just thinking about last year made me growl.

"Well, if we don't scare them at a Hallowe'en party, where do we scare them?" Walker asked, tapping out a rhythm with his fingers on the desk.

"Shane and I have some really good ideas," Shana said.

"Yeah. I think you have to listen to Shana and me this year," Shane chimed in. "We have a really good plan. It will have them shaking for a year. Really!"

Walker pulled the desk chair closer. Shane sat on the floor beside him. I leaned closer to Shana on the bed.

Speaking in a low voice just above a whisper, Shana told Walker and me their plan. A very scary plan.

It gave me a chill just hearing Shana describe it.

"It's very simple," Shana finished. "Very easy to do. And there's no way it won't work."

"We'll give Tabby and Lee a Hallowe'en they'll never forget!" Shane boasted.

"It's really mean," Walker murmured.

I gazed at the chubby, pink-cheeked twins. They were so cute-looking. So sweet and innocent. But their plan to frighten Tabby and Lee really was truly horrifying!

"It's mean," I agreed. "And it's cruel. And it's terribly gross and shocking." I grinned. "I *like* it!"

We all laughed.

"So we agree?" Shane asked. "We're doing it?"

We all agreed. We all solemnly shook hands.

"Great," Shana declared. "So Drew, all you have to do is invite them to come trick-or-treating with you. Shane and I will do the rest."

"No problem," I replied, still grinning. "No problem."

We all cheered and congratulated each other. We knew this was the year—*our* year.

Shana started to say something else—but my mum poked her head into the room.

"What are you four plotting so seriously?" Mum asked.

"Uh . . . nothing," Walker answered quickly.

"Just making plans for Hallowe'en, Mum," I told her.

Mum bit her lower lip. Her expression turned

serious. "You know, Drew," she said, shaking her head, "I don't think I can let you go trick-or-treating this year."

"Mum—you *have* to let me go trick-or-treating! You *have* to! Or else you'll spoil all of our plans for revenge!"

Those words *almost* burst from my mouth.

But somehow I held them in.

I choked back the words and stared hard at her, trying to decide if she was serious.

She was.

"Mum—what's wrong?" I finally cried. "What did I do? Why am I grounded?"

"Drew, you're not grounded." Mum laughed. "I just don't think trick-or-treating is a good idea this year. Haven't you seen the news stories? About the people in town who've disappeared?"

"Huh? Disappeared?"

My mind flashed back to my day-dream. I pictured the old couple again, locking kids up in their back room.

"You mean kids have disappeared?" I asked.

Mum shook her head. "No. Not kids. Adults.

A fourth person was reported missing yesterday. Here. Look."

Mum had the newspaper rolled up under her arm. She pulled it out and unrolled it. She held the front page up so we could all see it.

I could read the bold, black headline from across the room:

LOCAL MYSTERY: 4 HAVE VANISHED

I climbed up from the bed and made my way over to Mum. I saw Shane and Shana exchange worried glances. Walker's expression had turned solemn. He drummed his fingers tensely on the desktop.

I took the newspaper from Mum and stared at the photos of the four people who had disappeared. Three men and one woman.

"The police are warning people to be very careful," Mum said softly.

Walker walked over and took the newspaper from my hands. He studied the photos for a moment. "Hey—these people are all fat!" he exclaimed.

Now we all clustered around the paper and stared at the grey photos. Walker was right. All four people were very overweight. The first one, a bald man in a bulging turtleneck sweater, had at least six chins!

"Weird," I murmured.

Shane and Shana had grown strangely silent. I guessed they were frightened.

"Why would four fat people disappear into thin air?" Walker asked.

Mum sighed. "That's what the police would like to know," she said.

"But, Mum, if only adults are disappearing, why can't I go trick-or-treating?" I asked.

"Please let Drew go," Shana pleaded. "It's our last year to go out on Hallowe'en night."

"No. I don't think so," Mum replied, biting her bottom lip again.

"But we'll be *really really really* careful!" I promised her.

"I don't think so," Mum repeated. "I don't think so."

Once again, Hallowe'en was completely ruined.

But then Dad thought maybe trick-or-treating would be okay.

It was two days later. He and Mum had been discussing it non-stop.

"You can go out if you go in a group," Dad said. "Stay in the neighbourhood. And don't wander away from the others. Okay, Elf?"

"Thanks, Dad!" I cried. I was so happy, I didn't remind him to stop calling me Elf! Instead, I surprised him with a big hug.

"Are you sure about this?" Mum asked.

"Of course he is!" I cried.

There was no way I was going to let them change their minds. I was already halfway to the phone to tell Walker that our plan was back on!

"There will be a thousand kids trick-or-treating in the neighbourhood," Dad argued. "Besides, Drew and her friends are old enough and smart enough to keep out of trouble."

"Thanks, Dad!" I cried again.

Mum wanted to keep the discussion going. But I ran out of the kitchen and up to my room before she could get a word out.

I called Walker and told him the good news. He said he would call Shane and Shana and tell them to get ready for trick-or-treat night.

Everything was set. I had just one little problem left.

I had to convince Tabby and Lee that they should go trick-or-treating with us.

I took a deep breath and called Tabby's house. Her mother said she was over at Lee's, helping him get his Hallowe'en costume ready.

So I hurried over to Lee's house. It was a grey Saturday afternoon. It had rained all morning, and the storm clouds still floated overhead.

The front lawns shimmered from the clinging rainwater. I jumped over wide puddles on the pavement. I wore a heavy grey tracksuit. But the air felt damp and cold, and I wished I had put on a jacket over it.

I jogged the last block to Lee's house, partly to warm up. I stopped to catch my breath on the front doorstep. Then I pushed the doorbell.

A few seconds later, Lee answered the door.

"Whoa!" I cried out when I saw his costume. He had bobbing antennae on his head. He wore a fuzzy yellow waistcoat, pulled over a black-and-yellow-striped girl's swimsuit.

"You—you're a bee?" I stammered.

He nodded. "Tabby and I are still working on it. We bought black tights for my legs this morning."

"Cool," I said. He looked really stupid.

But why should I tell him?

Tabby greeted me as I stepped into the play-room. She had opened the package containing the tights and was stretching them out, tugging them hard between her hands.

"Drew—have you lost weight?" she asked.

"Excuse me? No."

"Oh. I suppose you *like* your tracksuit baggy like that—huh?"

She's so mean.

She turned her head away. But I saw her snig-ger to herself. She thinks she's really funny.

"Is that your costume?" she asked.

I decided to ignore her nasty jokes. "No. I'm going to be some kind of superhero, I think," I told her. "You know. Wear a cape and tights. What are you going to be?"

"A ballerina," she replied. She handed the tights to Lee. "Here are your bee legs. Do you have some heavy construction paper?"

"What for?" Lee asked.

"We need to make the stinger. You know. To glue to the back of your tights."

"No way!" Lee protested. "No stinger. I don't need a stinger. I'll only sit on it anyway."

I let them argue for a few minutes. I kept out of it.

Lee finally won. No stinger.

Tabby pouted for a while and made faces at him. She hates it when she doesn't get her way. But he's even more stubborn than she is.

"Listen, guys," I started, "Walker and Shane and Shana and I are all going to trick-or-treat together this year." I took a deep breath, then asked my question. "Want to come with us?"

"Yeah. Sure," Lee replied.

"Okay," Tabby agreed.

And that was that.

The trap was set.

Tabby and Lee were in for the most frightening Hallowe'en of their lives.

Unfortunately, we were, too.

The week dragged by. I counted the hours till Hallowe'en.

Finally, the big night arrived. I was so nervous, I could barely get my superhero costume together.

It wasn't much of a costume. I wore bright blue tights and a blue top. I pulled a pair of red boxer shorts over the tights.

For my cape, I cut up a red tablecloth we didn't use any more and tied it around my shoulders. Then I pulled on a pair of white vinyl boots. I had a red cardboard mask that just covered my eyes.

"Super Drew!" I proclaimed to the mirror.

I knew the costume was lame. But I didn't care. Tonight wasn't about costumes. It was about terror. It was about scaring two kids to death!

I grabbed a large brown shopping bag from the cupboard to use as a trick-or-treat bag. Then

I scrambled down the stairs, hoping to get out of the house before running into my parents. I hoped to avoid a last-minute lecture about how I had to be careful outside.

No such luck.

Dad stopped me at the bottom of the stairs. "Wow! Great costume, Elf!" he exclaimed. "What are you supposed to be?"

"Please don't call me Elf," I muttered. I tried to get past him to the front door, but he blocked my way.

"Just let me take one photo," he said.

"I'm a bit late," I told him. I was supposed to meet Walker on the corner at seven-thirty. It was already a quarter to eight.

"Be careful out there!" my mother called from the study.

Dad disappeared to get his camera. I waited at the bottom of the stairs, tapping my hand on the banister.

"Don't talk to any strangers!" Mum called.

Very helpful.

"Okay. One quick shot," Dad said, returning with his camera raised to his eye. "Stand against the door. You look great, Drew. Are you Wonder Woman or something?"

"Just a superhero," I mumbled. "I've really got to go, Dad."

He steadied the camera over his eye. "How about a smile?"

I gave him a toothy grin.

He clicked the shutter.

"Oh. Wait. Did it flash?" he asked. "I don't think I had the flash on." He examined the camera.

"Dad—" I started. I thought about Walker, standing by himself on the corner. Walker hated waiting. I knew how tense he'd be.

As tense as me.

"Dad, I've got to meet my friends."

"If you see anyone suspicious, run away!" Mum called from the study.

"Let's try again, Elf." Dad raised the camera again. "Smile."

He clicked the shutter. No flash.

"Whoa—" He checked the camera again.

"Dad, please—" I begged.

"Oh, wow," he murmured. "Would you believe it? No film." He shook his head. "I thought I had film in here. I'll go upstairs and get a roll. It will only take a second."

"Dad—!" I screamed.

The doorbell rang. It startled us both.

"Probably some trick-or-treaters," Dad said.

I leapt to the door and pulled it open. I squinted into the yellow porch light. A boy stood there all in black. He wore a black sweater and black trousers. A black wool ski cap was pulled down over his forehead. He had black make-up covering his face. And he wore black gloves.

"Cute costume," Dad declared. "Get him some sweets, Drew."

I groaned. "Dad, it's not a trick-or-treater. It's Walker." I pushed open the storm door so that Walker could come in.

"I thought you were going to meet me," he said.

Dad stared at Walker's all-black costume. "What are you supposed to be?" he asked.

"A dark and stormy night," Walker replied.

"Huh? Where's the stormy part?" I asked.

"Here," Walker replied. He raised a black plastic water pistol and squirted me in the face.

Dad burst out laughing. He thought that was a riot. He called Mum in from the study to take a look.

"We're never getting out of here," I whispered to Walker. "We're going to miss Tabby and Lee."

We had the night all planned out, down to the minute. But now the whole plan could be ruined.

I had a knot in my stomach. I could feel it tightening. The cape suddenly felt as if it were choking me.

Mum and Dad were admiring Walker's costume. "A dark and stormy night! Very clever," Mum said. "But how will anyone see you in the dark? You'd better be very careful crossing the street."

Mum had advice for everyone tonight.

I couldn't take it any more. "We've got to go.

298

Bye," I said. I shoved Walker out the door and followed right behind him.

Mum called out more warnings from the house. But I couldn't hear her. I pulled Walker down the driveway, and we hurried towards the corner. That's where we were supposed to meet Tabby and Lee.

Our two victims.

"You should have stayed on the corner," I scolded Walker. "Maybe Tabby and Lee have been here already and left."

"But you were so late," Walker protested. "I thought maybe something was wrong."

My heart was thumping. The knot in my stomach grew even tighter. "Okay, okay," I urged. "Let's just calm down."

It was a clear, cold night. A light frost made the lawns silvery. Overhead, a sliver of moon rested near a cluster of bright stars.

Most of the houses on the block had their lights on. I saw two groups of little trick-or-treaters across the street. They were all hurrying up to the same house. A dog barked excitedly in the house next door.

I turned my eyes to the corner where we were supposed to meet Tabby and Lee. No one there.

Walker and I stopped under the street light. I adjusted my cape. It was really choking me. I saw that I hadn't cut it short enough. The bottom was soaked from dragging along the ground.

"Where are they?" I demanded.

"You know they're always late," Walker replied.

He was right. Tabby and Lee loved to keep people waiting for them.

"They will be here any second," Walker said.

A tall hedge ran along the corner garden. Walker started pacing back and forth from the hedge to the kerb. His outfit was so black, when he stepped into the shadow of the hedge, he completely disappeared!

"Could you stop pacing—?" I started.

But my voice caught in my throat when I heard a cough. From the other side of the hedge.

A low, gruff cough.

Not a human cough. More like an animal growl.

I turned and saw that Walker had heard it, too. He stopped pacing and stared at the hedge.

I heard a scraping sound. The hedge appeared to shiver.

"Wh-who's back there?" I choked out.

The hedge shook again. Shook and cracked.

"Hey—who *is* it?" Walker cried.

Silence.

The hedge shook. Harder this time.

"Is this a joke or something?" Walker demanded in a trembling voice.

Another low animal growl.

"Noooo—!" I cried out as two ugly creatures came snarling through the hedge.

I saw only a blur of ragged fur. Open jaws. Saliva-covered teeth.

Before I could move, one of the creatures leapt on to me, snarling and growling. It shoved me roughly down to the grass. And dug its fangs into my shoulder.

I let out a shrill wail of pain.

I tried to scramble to my feet. But the snarling creature had me pinned to the ground.

"Stop! *Stop!*" I struggled to squirm free as the creature tugged my cape over me, covering me like a blanket.

"Hey—!" I heard Walker's angry shout. But I couldn't see what was happening to him.

"Noooooo! Let me go!" I shrieked.

With a frantic burst of energy, I reached up one hand—and swiped at the creature's drooling face.

To my shock, the whole face pulled off easily.

A mask. I held a rubber mask in my hand.

I stared up at a grinning face.

It took me a few moments to recognize the boy. Todd Jeffrey. Yes. Todd Jeffrey, the high-school kid who had frightened us all at Lee's party two years ago.

"Todd," I murmured. I frantically pulled the cape away from my face.

"Gotcha! Gotcha good!" he whispered. He let go of me and stood up.

"You creep!" I cried angrily. I tossed the rubber mask in his face.

He caught it in one hand and laughed. "Drew, can't you take a joke?"

"Huh? A joke? A *joke*?" I screamed.

I climbed to my feet and furiously began brushing myself off. My cape was totally tangled and covered with wet brown leaves.

Walker had been wrestling with the other creature. The guy pulled off his mask. Of course it was Joe, Todd's disgusting friend.

"Hope we didn't *scare* you!" he teased. He and Todd laughed like hyenas. They fell all over each other, slapping high fives and low fives.

Before I could tell them what jerks they were, I heard more laughter. To my surprise, Tabby and Lee came stepping out from behind the hedge. And all four of them enjoyed a good laugh together.

"Grrrrrrr!" I uttered a furious growl. At that moment, I wished I really *were* a superhero. I wanted to plough my superfists into their laughing faces.

Or maybe spread my cape and fly away—far away, so I wouldn't have to see any of them any more.

"Happy Hallowe'en, Drew!" Tabby called smugly.

"Happy Hallowe'en!" Tabby and Lee repeated in unison, grinning their disgusting grins.

"How long were you and Lee standing back there?" I demanded angrily.

"Long enough!" Lee sniggered. He and Tabby both burst out laughing again.

"We were standing back there the whole time," Tabby declared. "I *love* Hallowe'en—don't you?"

I growled under my breath. But I didn't say anything.

Keep cool, Drew, I instructed myself. Tabby and Lee and their two high-school buddies played a little joke on you.

But they won't have the last laugh.

When the night is over, I told myself, Walker and I will be the ones who are laughing.

When Shane and Shana arrive, we are going to terrify them. Truly terrify them.

Todd and Joe had pulled their monster masks back on. They tilted back their heads and howled like wolves. Todd's mask was really gross. It had rubber saliva dripping over the long, pointy fangs.

"They're not coming trick-or-treating with us—are they?" I asked Tabby.

Tabby shook her head. She adjusted the tiara on top of her blonde hair.

"No way!" Todd replied from behind the ugly mask. "Joe and I are too old to trick-or-treat. Especially with you crybabies."

"Then why are you wearing those monster costumes?" Walker demanded.

"Just to scare kids," Joe replied. He and Todd laughed again, loud, cruel laughs.

Joe grabbed my mask and pulled it down to my chin. Todd rubbed the back of his hand over Walker's cheek, smearing the black make-up. Then they ran off to find some other victims.

What creeps.

I was glad to see them go. I stood watching them, making sure they didn't change their minds and come back.

"Nice guys," Lee said. He set his orange and black trick-or-treat bag down on the grass. Then he adjusted his bee antennae.

I heard kids laughing across the street. I turned and saw a group of four kids—all monsters and goblins—running up the driveway to a house.

"Let's get going," Tabby said. "It's getting cold."

"Aren't Shane and Shana supposed to meet us?" Lee asked.

"Yeah. They'll catch us up," I said.

We crossed the street and started towards the first house, a tall, brightly lit brick house with a smiling pumpkin cut-out in the front window.

As we made our way up the gravel driveway,
I glanced at my watch.

And gasped.

Nearly eight-fifteen.

Shane and Shana were supposed to meet us
on the corner at eight.

Where *were* they?

They were never late. Never.

I swallowed hard.

Was this Hallowe'en about to be ruined, too?

Had something gone wrong?

We stepped up on to the front doorstep and peered through the glass storm door. A big orange cat with bright blue eyes stared back at us from the other side of the door.

I rang the doorbell.

A few seconds later, a smiling young woman in jeans and a yellow turtleneck came hurrying to the door. She carried a basket of Snickers bars and Milky Ways.

"You all look great," she declared, dropping a chocolate bar in each bag.

"Drew—hold up your bag!" Tabby ordered shrilly.

"Oh. Sorry." I was still worrying about Shane and Shana. I held up my bag for the woman. The cat narrowed its amazing blue eyes at me.

"Are you supposed to be a princess?" the woman asked Tabby.

"No. A ballerina," Tabby replied.

"And you're a lump of coal?" the woman asked Walker.

"Something like that," Walker muttered. He didn't do his dark-and-stormy-night routine. I guessed he was worried about Shane and Shana, too.

"Have fun," the woman said. She pulled the storm door shut.

The four of us jumped off her doorstep and started across the frost-covered grass to the next house. When I glanced back to the door, I saw the cat still staring out at us.

The next house was dark. So we crossed the lawn to the house next door to it. A group of kids was already on the front doorstep, shouting, "Trick or treat! Trick or treat!"

"Where *are* they?" I whispered to Walker.

He shrugged.

"If they don't show up . . ." I started. But I saw Tabby watching me. So I didn't finish my sentence.

We waited for the kids to leave, then climbed up to the doorstep. Two little kids—probably three or four years old—were handing out little bags of sweets to everyone.

The laughed at Lee's bee costume. They wanted to feel the antennae. The little boy asked Lee where his stinger was.

"I stuck it in someone," Lee told him.

They stared hard at Walker's all-black outfit.

I think it kind of frightened them. "Are you supposed to be a monster?" the little girl asked Walker timidly.

"No. I'm a lump of coal," Walker told her.

She nodded seriously.

We hurried away and did three more houses to the end of the block. I saw two kids that I babysit for. They were in matching robot costumes. I stopped to talk with them for a minute.

Then I had to run to catch up with the others. They had crossed the street and had started doing the houses on the other side.

A strong gust of wind fluttered my cape. I shivered—and glanced nervously at my watch again.

Where were they? Where *were* Shane and Shana?

The whole plan depended on them . . .

"Wow! Pretty good haul so far!" Lee declared. He held his bag open, studying the contents as we crossed the street.

"Did you get any Kit Kats?" Tabby demanded. "I'll trade anyone for Kit Kats."

"Only one person gave out apples," Lee said, making a disgusted face. He reached into his bag and pulled out the apple. Then he heaved it as hard as he could across the garden.

The apple hit a tree trunk with a loud *thunk*. Then it bounced into the next driveway.

"Why do people give out apples?" Lee

grumbled. "Don't they know we only want sweets?"

"Some people are just cheap," Tabby said. She pulled out her apple and dropped it in the grass. Then she kicked it with the toe of her ballet slipper.

They both really deserve what they're going to get, I thought. They're both really jerks.

But where are Shane and Shana?

We trick-or-treated our way down the block. It was getting pretty late, and there were fewer little kids out.

The street light near the corner was broken. We stepped into a patch of deep shadow.

One of Lee's antennae kept slipping off. He slid it back into place for the tenth time.

As we neared the corner, a tall tree blocked the moonlight, and it grew even darker.

"Oh—!" I let out a cry as two figures leapt out at us from behind the tree.

I thought that Todd and Joe had returned.

But I quickly saw that it wasn't those guys.

In a grey blur, the two figures turned their backs on us, blocking our way. They wore dark robes that flowed straight down to the ground. And over their heads . . .

Over their heads . . .

They wore pumpkins!

Large, round pumpkins, perfectly balanced on their shoulders.

310

"Whoa—!" Walker let out a startled cry. He backed up and stumbled into me.

Tabby and Lee gaped in surprise.

But the most horrifying surprise was yet to come.

As they slowly turned to face us, their jack-o'-lantern faces came into view.

Eerie, jagged grins cut into their pumpkin heads.

Flashing triangle eyes.

Lit by flames!

Bright orange and yellow flames danced inside their heads!

And as the pumpkin heads turned their fiery, ragged grins on us, Walker and I opened our mouths and screamed in terror.

Our screams echoed down the block.

The fire flashed in the pumpkin heads' eyes.

I turned to Tabby and Lee. The light from the fiery jack-o'-lantern faces flickered over their faces. They stood calmly, staring at the grinning pumpkin heads.

Tabby turned to me. "Is this your idea of a joke? Were you trying to scare us?"

"We *know* it's Shane and Shana," Lee said. He tugged at one of the dark, loose, flowing costumes. "Hey, Shane—how's it going?"

The two pumpkin heads remained silent.

"How did you get the fire to work? Do you have candles in there?" Tabby demanded. "How can you see?"

The pumpkin heads grinned back in silence. A lick of fire darted out from one of the jagged mouths.

I shivered. These costumes were *too* good. I could hear the flames hiss inside the big orange heads. The costumes were dark green, like pumpkin vines.

Why aren't Tabby and Lee frightened? I wondered.

I expected Shane and Shana to appear in something frightening. But I didn't expect anything as good as these fiery jack-o'-lantern heads.

The costumes were great. But I felt so disappointed. Tabby and Lee were definitely not frightened.

This Hallowe'en is going to be a disaster—like the others, I thought.

I stepped up beside Walker. I couldn't see his expression under all that black make-up.

"How do they do the fire?" he whispered. "It's really awesome!"

I nodded. "But it didn't scare Tabby and Lee," I whispered back.

"It's early," Walker whispered. "Shane and Shana have just started."

My cape had become tangled around my legs. I tugged it free and tossed it behind me.

The two pumpkin heads still hadn't said a word.

Tabby picked up her trick-or-treat bag and turned to me. "You'll have to do better than this if you want to scare Lee and me," she said with a sneer.

"We're not scaredy-cats like you two," Lee boasted.

313

Flames darted out of the pumpkin heads' eyes. They both tilted their big heads as they stared at Tabby and Lee.

How do they do that? I wondered. How do they control the flames? Do they have some kind of remote control?

"Well, are we going to stand here and freeze? Or are we going to trick-or-treat?" Tabby demanded.

"Let's do *your* block," I suggested to her.

Tabby started to reply—but a hiss of fire from the nearest pumpkin head made her stop.

"Let's go somewhere else," the jack-o'-lantern said from somewhere inside the pumpkin head. His voice came out in a hoarse crackle. Too harsh to be a whisper. A dry, choked sound.

"Somewhere else," his partner echoed. Her voice also come out in a hoarse crackle. Like dry, dead leaves being crinkled together.

"Excuse me?" Lee cried.

"We know a better neighbourhood," the first pumpkin head crackled. The jagged mouth, cut through the thick pumpkin flesh, didn't move. The voice hissed from inside. The orange and yellow flames tossed in rhythm to the words.

"We know a better neighbourhood."

"A neighbourhood you won't forget."

Tabby laughed. She rolled her eyes. "Oh, wow. Scary voices!" she said sarcastically.

"Oooh, I'm shaking! I'm shaking!" Lee teased.

He and Tabby laughed together.

"Give us a break, guys," Tabby said to the pumpkin heads. "Your costumes are pretty good. But they didn't scare us. So lose the creepy voices, okay?"

"Yeah," Lee agreed. "Let's do some houses. It's getting late."

"*Follow ussss*," one of the pumpkin heads hissed.

"*Follow us to a new neighbourhood. A better neighbourhood.*"

They led the way down the street. Their big heads bounced on their shoulders as they walked. The fire flickered from their heads, casting a glow like lighted torches.

"What are they doing?" Walker whispered in my ear. "This isn't in the plan. Where are they taking us?"

I didn't know.

We walked three blocks, heading away from our houses. We passed a row of big stone houses set back on wide lawns behind tall hedges. The next block had an empty plot where someone had started to build a house, and then stopped.

The two pumpkin heads walked quickly, taking long strides. Their heads bounced on their shoulders. They kept their fiery faces straight ahead and didn't glance back at us.

"Where are we going?" Lee demanded, jogging to catch up with them. He tugged at one of their shoulders. "You're passing a lot of good houses across the street."

The jack-o'-lantern creature didn't slow down. *"Let's try a new neighbourhood,"* he crackled.

"Yessssss," his partner hissed. *"A new neighbourhood. A better neighbourhood. You'll see."*

They led us past the empty plot. Past a row of small, dark houses.

"Where are we going?" Walker whispered. He motioned to Shane and Shana. "What is their problem? Why are they doing this? They're starting to scare *me*!"

"I'm sure they know what they're doing," I whispered back.

I gazed around the block. I didn't see many other trick-or-treaters. It was getting late, and most of the little kids had already gone home.

In the next driveway, two tall kids—a gorilla and a chubby clown—were pawing through their trick-or-treat bags. They had their heads lowered to the bags. We passed by them, and they didn't even look up.

"Hey—we're missing a lot of good houses!" Lee protested. He pointed to a brick house on the corner. "Can we stop there? Those people always give out handfuls of sweets. Really. Handfuls!"

The pumpkin heads ignored him and kept walking.

"Hey—whoa! Stop!" Tabby demanded.

She and Lee both trotted up in front of the pumpkin heads.

"Stop! Come on—whoa!"

"*A new neighbourhood*," one of them croaked.

"*Let's try a new neighbourhood*," the other one echoed.

"*A better neighbourhood*."

A chill ran down my back. Shane and Shana were acting so *weird*.

I tugged my cape off a clump of weeds. The air suddenly felt colder, and damp. I wrapped the cape around me.

Up ahead, Lee fiddled with his bee antennae. I saw that Tabby's ballet slippers were soaked with mud.

We followed the pumpkin heads across the street. And then they stepped off the pavement and started to walk into a dark wood.

Walker hurried up beside me. Even through his heavy make-up, I could see the worried expression on his face. "Why are they taking us into the wood?" he whispered.

I shrugged. "I suppose they're getting ready to scare Tabby and Lee."

Twigs and dead leaves crackled under our shoes as we made our way between the trees.

A frightening thought flashed into my mind. I suddenly pictured the four fat people who had disappeared.

Four people. Vanished into thin air. Never seen again.

I remembered all of my mother's warnings. I remembered how she told us to stay where there were a lot of kids and a lot of bright lights.

I remembered how she didn't even want me to go trick-or-treating tonight.

This is wrong, I realized.

Mum's advice was smart. We shouldn't be walking through the woods tonight, I knew.

We shouldn't be away from the street, away from the brightly lit houses.

We shouldn't go off by ourselves like this in the dark, creepy woods.

"*A new neighbourhood*," a pumpkin head crackled from up ahead.

"*Just past these woods*," the other one whispered. "*A really good neighbourhood. You'll see.*"

The light from inside their heads flickered over the dark tangles of bare trees and tall weeds.

My heart began to thud. I hurried to keep up with the others.

Shane and Shana are good friends, I told myself.

I'm sure they know where they're going.

But this isn't what we planned. This isn't what we planned at all.

Why do I have such a bad feeling about this?

"Shane! Shana! Give us a break!" Tabby complained shrilly. "Look at me! Look at my ballerina skirt!"

She held up the front of the skirt. Even in the dim light, I could see the mud stain on the front.

"We have to get out of these woods!" Tabby wailed angrily.

"Yeah. It's too dark. And we're wasting too much time," Lee agreed.

His trick-or-treat bag got caught on a low tree branch. He tugged it hard to pull it loose.

Shane and Shana ignored the complaints. The big, fiery pumpkins bouncing on their shoulders, they made their way steadily and quickly through the darkness of the woods.

A few minutes later, we stepped out on to a narrow street. Seeing the bright street lights and rows of little houses, we all let out a happy cheer.

"*Now we can trick-or-treat,*" one of the pump-kin heads croaked.

I turned my eyes up and down the street. I saw house after house, all small, all on tiny lawns. Most of them had lights on in front. Many of them were decorated for Hallowe'en.

The houses stretched for blocks. Two rows of brightly lit little houses—as far as I could see.

"This *is* an awesome neighbourhood for trick-or-treating!" I declared, starting to feel a lot better. A lot less frightened.

"Excellent!" Lee agreed. "We'll clean up here!"

"Where are we?" Walker demanded. "How come I've never seen this neighbourhood before?"

No one answered him. We were all too eager to get started.

I pulled some wet leaves off my cape and straightened my mask. Tramping through the woods had messed all of us up. We took a few seconds to get our costumes in better shape.

Then the six of us hurried up to the first house.

A young woman carrying a baby in one arm came to the door. She dropped miniature choc-olate bars into our bags. The baby stared at the flaming pumpkin heads and smiled.

At the next house, an elderly couple took for ever getting to the door. "Trick or treat!" we shouted at the top of our lungs. They raised their hands to their ears. I don't think they could stand the noise.

"I'm sorry. But we don't have any sweets," the old woman said. She dropped nickels into our bags. A nickel per bag.

We hurried across the small garden to the next house. Two girls, about seven or eight, greeted us at the door. "Awesome costumes!" one of them said to Shane and Shana. They gave us little bags of M&M's.

"This is cool!" Lee declared as we hurried to the next house.

"The houses are so close together," Tabby added. "We can do a hundred houses in no time!"

"Why haven't we ever come here before?" Walker asked.

"Trick or treat!" we screamed as we rang the doorbell on the next house.

A teenaged boy with long blond hair and an earring in one ear answered the door. He sniggered at our costumes. "Cool," he muttered. Then he dropped packets of sweets into our bags.

On to the next house. And the next and the next.

We did the next block, stopping at every house. Then we covered two more blocks. The little houses seemed to stretch on forever.

My trick-or-treat bag was nearly full. We stopped at the corner because Walker's shoe had come untied. While he bent down to tie it, we all stopped to catch our breath.

"*Hurry up!*" a pumpkin urged Walker. Flames leapt angrily from his eyeholes.

"*Yesssss, hurry,*" the other one hissed. "*No time to wasssssste.*"

"Give me a break," Walker murmured. "I have a knot."

As he struggled with his shoe, the two pumpkin heads bobbed and squirmed impatiently.

Finally, Walker climbed to his feet and picked up his bulging trick-or-treat bag. The pumpkin heads were already leading the way to the next block of houses.

"I'm getting a little tired," I heard Lee whisper to Tabby. "What time is it?"

"My bag is nearly full," Tabby replied. With a groan, she shifted the heavy bag to her other hand.

"*Hurry,*" a pumpkin head insisted. "*Lots more houses to do.*"

"*Lotsssssss,*" the other one hissed.

We did two more blocks. Both sides of the street. About twenty houses.

My bag was filled to the top. I had to carry it in both hands.

Walker's shoelace had come undone again. When he bent to tie it, it ripped in his hand. "*Now* what am I going to do?" he muttered.

"*Hurry,*" a pumpkin head insisted.

"*More houses.*"

"I'm getting tired," Tabby complained, loud enough for everyone to hear this time.

"Me, too," Lee agreed. "And this trick-or-treat bag is getting heavy."

"Stupid shoelace," Walker muttered, still bent over his shoe.

"I suppose it *is* getting pretty late," I said, gazing around. "I don't see any other trick-or-treaters. I think they've all gone home."

I pulled off my cape. It was all tangled, and it was starting to choke me. I balled it up and tucked it under my arm.

"*More houses,*" one of the pumpkin heads whispered.

"*Hurry. Lots more to do,*" the other one insisted in her dry, crackling voice. The yellow flames danced inside her head.

"But we want to quit!" Lee whined.

"Yes. We're done," Tabby agreed shrilly.

"*You can't quit!*" a pumpkin head snapped.

"Huh?" Lee's mouth dropped open.

"*Keep going! You can't quit!*" the pumpkin head insisted.

They both appeared to float up, to rise up over us. The fires raged in their triangle eyes. The heads floated up over the dark, caped bodies.

"*You can't quit! You can't EVER quit!*"

"Ha-ha. Very funny." Tabby rolled her eyes.

But I saw Lee step back in fear. His knees seemed to buckle, and he nearly dropped his trick-or-treat bag.

"*Another block*," a pumpkin head insisted.

"*Another block. And then another.*"

"Whoa. Wait a minute!" Tabby protested. "You can't boss us around like that. I'm going home."

She turned and started to walk away. But the two pumpkin heads moved quickly to block her path.

"Let me go!" Tabby protested.

She darted sharply to the right. But the big pumpkin creatures floated with her. Their fiery grins appeared to grow wider. Brighter.

The two of them began circling us, floating silently. They swirled around us, faster and faster—until it looked as if we were surrounded by flames.

A wall of leaping flames all around us!

"*You will obey!*" came the crackling command.

The flames pushed up from behind. Forced us forward.

We had no choice but to obey them. We were prisoners. Prisoners of their fire.

An old man was standing at the door to the first house. He grinned at us as we stepped on to his front doorstep. "You kids are out pretty late—aren't you?" he asked.

"Fairly," I replied.

He dropped packets of Chuckles into our bags.

"*Hurry*," a pumpkin head urged as we crossed the wet grass to the next house. "*Hurry!*"

Lee's trick-or-treat bag was so heavy, he dragged it along the ground. I carried mine in both hands. Tabby complained to herself, muttering and shaking her head.

We did both sides of the block. I didn't see any other kids out. No cars came by. Some of the houses were turning out their lights.

"*Hurry!*" a pumpkin head insisted.

"*Lots more houses. Lots more blocks.*"

"No way!" Lee cried.

"No way!" Tabby repeated. She tried to sound strong. But I heard a tremble in her voice.

The jack-o'-lantern faces loomed over us once again. The fiery eyes stared out at us.

"Hurry. You can't stop now! You CAN'T!"

"But it's too late!" I protested.

"And my shoe keeps coming off," Walker chimed in.

"We don't want to trick-or-treat any more," Tabby told them shrilly.

"You can't stop now! Hurry!"

"Lots more houses. This is the BEST neighbourhood!"

"No way!" Tabby and Lee repeated together. They started to chant. "No way! No way! No way!"

"Our bags are full," I said.

"Mine is starting to tear," Walker complained.

"No way! No way!" Tabby and Lee chanted.

The two jack-o'-lanterns began to swirl around us again, circling faster and faster, rebuilding the wall of flames. *"You mussssst not ssssstop!"* one of them hissed.

"You musssst keep going!"

They swirled closer. So close I could feel the scorching heat of their flames.

And as they swirled, they began to hiss, like snakes about to strike.

The hissing grew louder, louder—until it sounded as if we were *surrounded* by snakes!

My heavy trick-or-treat bag fell from my hands. "Stop—!" I screamed at them. "Stop it! You're not Shane and Shana!"

Fire leapt from their eyes. Their hisses became a high wail.

"You're not Shane and Shana!" I shrieked. "Who are you?"

They swirled to a stop. Bright flames licked out of their grinning mouths. Their shrill wails bounced off the bare trees, cutting through the heavy night silence.

"Who are you?" I demanded again, my voice trembling. My whole body shook. I suddenly felt as if the cold of the night had seeped inside me.

"Who are you? Have you done something to our friends?"

No reply.

I turned to Walker. The light of the flames flickered over his face. Through his black make-up, I could see his frightened expression.

I swallowed hard and turned to Tabby and Lee. They were both sneering and shaking their heads.

"Is this your idea of a stupid Hallowe'en joke?" Tabby demanded. She rolled her eyes. "Wow. Did you really think Lee and I would fall for this?"

"Ooh—I'm scared! I'm scared!" Lee cried sarcastically. He made his knees knock together. "Look—I'm shaking like a leaf!"

He and Tabby let out loud laughs.

"These are really clever costumes. Great fire effects. But we know it's Shane and Shana," Lee declared. "There's no way you're going to scare us, Drew."

"No way," Tabby repeated. "Look—!"

She and Lee reached out their hands. They each grabbed a pumpkin head—and tugged.

"Whoa!"

They pulled the fiery pumpkin heads off the creatures' shoulders.

And then all four of us screamed—because the two costumed figures *had no heads underneath*!

Our screams rose up shrilly, cutting through the night air like wailing sirens.

The pumpkin head fell from Tabby's hand and bounced heavily on the ground. Bright orange flames shot out of its eyes and mouth.

Lee still gripped the other pumpkin head between his hands. But he dropped it when the jagged mouth began to move.

The fiery heads grinned up at us from the grass.

"Ohhh." I uttered a low moan of terror and staggered back. I wanted to run away, to run as fast as I could and not look back.

But I couldn't take my eyes off the two heads, grinning up at us from the wet grass.

As I stared, my heart pounded and my legs began to shake. Someone grabbed my arm.

"Walker!"

He held on to me. His hand was as cold as

ice. With his other hand, he pointed to the two headless bodies.

They stood in their dark, flowing costumes. They hadn't moved. The spot between their shoulders where their heads had rested was flat and smooth.

As if the pumpkin heads had been balanced there. But never attached.

Never attached.

Tabby and Lee huddled together beside me. Tabby's tiara was missing. Her hair had come unpinned. It fell in wet tangles over her face.

Lee's trick-or-treat bag had toppled on to its side. A pile of sweets had spilled over the grass, centimetres away from one of the pumpkin heads.

The flames inside the heads danced and flickered. And then the jagged mouths began to move.

The smiles grew wider. The triangle eyes narrowed.

"Hee hee hee heeeeee."

An ugly laugh escaped their mouths. An evil, dry sound. More like a throat clearing, more like a cough than a laugh.

"Hee hee heeeeeeeee."

"Noooo!" I moaned. Beside me, I heard Walker gasp.

Lee swallowed hard. Tabby was holding on to the sleeve of his bee costume with both hands.

She pulled him back until they were standing behind Walker and me.

"*Hee hee heeeeeeeee.*"

The heads laughed together, flames flickering inside them.

Their two bodies moved quickly. They reached out long arms and grabbed the heads up from the grass.

I expected them to place the heads back on their shoulders. But they didn't. They held the heads in front of their chests.

"*Hee heeeeeee.*"

Another dry laugh. The pumpkin mouths twisted on the dark, round faces. The eyes stared blankly at us, bright orange, then shadowy, flickering with the flames.

I realized I was squeezing Walker's arm. He didn't even seem to notice.

I let go. And took a deep breath.

"Who are you?" I called to the two creatures. My voice came out high and tiny. "Who are you? And what do you want?"

"*Hee heee heeeee.*" They laughed their ugly laughs again.

"Who are you?" I choked out again, shouting over their dry, crackling laughter. "Where are Shane and Shana? Where are our friends?"

Flames hissed from the two heads. Their ragged orange grins grew wider.

"Drew—let's try one more time to run away," Walker whispered. "Maybe if we catch them by surprise . . ."

We both spun round and started to run. Tabby and Lee came stumbling after us.

My legs felt so wobbly and weak, I didn't think I could run. My heart pounded so hard, I struggled to breathe.

"Run!" Walker cried breathlessly, pulling my arm. "Drew—faster!"

We didn't get far.

Uttering their shrill, frightening hisses, the creatures whirled around us once again. Trapping us. Holding us prisoner inside their circle of flames.

No way we could run away. No way we could escape from them.

Peering over the flying flames, I searched desperately up and down the street.

No one in sight. Nothing moved. No cars. No people. Not even a dog or a cat.

Holding their heads at their waists, the two creatures stepped up to us. They stood over us menacingly, raising the red, glowing heads high above their bare shoulders.

"More houses. More houses." The jack-o'-lantern lips pushed out the words. The red eyes stared down at us.

"More houses. More houses."

"You cannot stop. You must keep on trick-or-treating!"

"Pick up your bags. Pick them up—now!" one of them growled. Her head held up between two hands, she gazed down at us, her jagged lips forming an evil sneer.

"We—we don't *want* to trick-or-treat!" Lee wailed, holding on to Tabby.

"We want to go home!" Tabby cried.

"More houses. More houses. More houses." The pumpkin heads continued their hissing chant.

They bumped us together. They bumped and pushed us.

We had no choice. Wearily, we picked up our trick-or-treat bags from where they had fallen on the grass.

They moved behind us, chanting, chanting in their low, dry whispers. *"More houses. More houses."*

They pushed us to the first house on the block. They pushed us on to the front doorstep. Then they hovered close behind.

"How—how long do we have to trick-or-treat?" Tabby demanded.

The pumpkin heads grinned together. *"For ever!"* they declared.

A woman came to the door and dropped packets of Hershey's kisses into our bags. "You kids are out awfully late," she said. "Do you live round here?"

"No," I replied. "We don't really know where we are. We're in a strange neighbourhood, and we're being forced to trick-or-treat by two headless pumpkin creatures. And they say they're going to make us trick-or-treat for ever. Help us—please! You've got to help us!"

"Ha-ha! That's good!" the woman laughed. "That's very funny. You have a very good imagination." She closed the door before I could get out another word.

At the next house, we didn't even bother to ask for help. We knew no one would believe us.

"Your bags are so full!" the woman exclaimed. "You must have been trick-or-treating for hours!"

"We . . . we really like sweets," Walker replied wearily.

I glanced back at the pumpkin heads. They were motioning impatiently. They wanted us to move on to the next house.

We said goodbye to the woman and made our way across the front garden. Our trick-or-treat bags were heavy, so we dragged them along the grass.

As we headed for the next driveway, Tabby hurried up beside me. "What are we going to do?" she whispered in my ear. "How are we going to get away from these . . . these *monsters*?"

I shrugged. I didn't know how to answer her.

"I'm so scared," Tabby confessed. "You don't think these pumpkin creatures really plan to make us trick-or-treat *for ever*—do you? What do they really want? Why are they doing this to us?"

"I don't know," I said, swallowing hard. I could see that Tabby was about to cry.

Lee was walking with his head down. He dragged his bulging trick-or-treat bag behind him. He was shaking his head, muttering to himself.

We stepped up to the next porch and rang the bell. A middle-aged man in bright yellow pyjamas opened the door. "Trick or treat!" we cried wearily.

He dropped little Tootsie Rolls into our bags.

"Very late," he muttered. "Do your parents know you're still out?"

We dragged on to the next house. And the next.

I kept waiting for a chance to escape. But the two creatures never let us out of their sight. They stayed right with us, keeping in the shadows. Their eyes glowed red from the deepening fire inside their heads.

"*More houses*," they chanted, forcing us to cross the street and do the long row of houses on the other side.

"*More houses.*"

"I'm so scared," Tabby repeated to me in a trembling whisper. "So is Lee. We're so scared, we feel sick."

I started to tell her I felt the same way.

But we both gasped when we saw someone walking along the street.

A man in a blue uniform!

At first I thought he was a policeman. But as he stepped under a street light, I saw that he wore a blue work uniform. He had a blue baseball cap on his head. He carried a large black lunch box in one hand.

He must be coming home from work, I told myself. He was whistling softly to himself, walking with his head down. I don't think he saw us.

Tabby changed that. "Helllllp!" she screamed. "Sir—please! Help us!"

The man raised his head, startled. He squinted at us.

Tabby began running across the grass to him. The rest of us followed, dragging our heavy trick-or-treat bags.

"Help us—please!" Tabby pleaded shrilly. "You've got to save us!"

The four of us hurtled breathlessly into the street. We surrounded the startled man. He narrowed his eyes at us and scratched his brown, curly hair.

"What's wrong, kids? Are you lost?" he asked.

"Monsters!" Lee exploded. "Headless jack-o'-lantern monsters! They've captured us! They're forcing us to trick-or-treat!"

The man started to laugh.

"No—it's true!" Tabby insisted. "You've got to believe us! You've got to help us!"

"Hurry!" Lee cried.

The man scratched his hair again. He squinted at us hard, studying our faces.

"Hurry! Please hurry!" Lee wailed.

I stared back at the startled man.

Would he help us?

"You've *got* to help us!" Lee pleaded.

"Okay. I'll go along with the joke," the man said, rolling his eyes. "Where are your monsters?"

"There!" I cried.

We all turned back to the front garden.

No one there. The pumpkin heads had gone. Disappeared.

Tabby gasped. Lee's mouth dropped open.

"Where did they go?" Walker murmured.

"They were standing right there!" Tabby insisted. "Both of them. Holding their heads in their hands! Really!"

The man let out a long sigh. "You kids have a good Hallowe'en," he said wearily. "But give me a break, okay? I've just got off work, and I'm beat."

He shifted his black lunch box to the other hand. Then we watched him make his way up the driveway. He disappeared round the back of the house.

"Let's get *out* of here!" Lee cried.

But before we could run, the two pumpkin heads leapt out from behind a low hedge. The red flames hissed inside their heads. Their jagged mouths were turned down in angry snarls.

"*More houses,*" they insisted, rasping the words together. "*More houses. You can't stop trick-or-treating.*"

"But we're so tired!" Tabby protested. Her voice cracked. Again, I saw tears wetting her eyes.

"Let us go—please!" Lee begged.

"*More houses. More!*"

"*You can never stop! NEVER!*"

"I can't!" Lee cried. "My bag is full. Look!" He held out the bulging trick-or-treat bag to the pumpkin heads. Sweets spilled over the top.

"Mine is full, too!" Walker declared. "It's filled to the top. I couldn't squeeze another Smartie in it!"

"We have to go home!" Tabby cried. "Our bags are totally full."

"*That's no problem,*" one of the pumpkin heads replied.

"No problem?" Tabby wailed. "No problem?"

"*Start eating,*" the pumpkin head ordered.

"Huh?" We all gasped.

"*Start eating*," he insisted. "*Start eating*."

"Hey—no way!" Lee protested. "We're not going to stand here and—"

The creatures appeared to rise up. Bright yellow flames shot out from their eyes. A roar of hot wind escaped their jagged, snarling mouths. The wind burned my face.

We all knew what would happen if we refused to do as they said. We'd end up inside the flames.

Lee grabbed a chocolate bar from the top of his trick-or-treat bag. He tore off the wrapper with a trembling hand. And he shoved it into his mouth.

We all started to eat. We had no choice.

I shoved a Hershey bar into my mouth and started to chew. I couldn't even taste it. A big gob stuck to my teeth. But I shoved in more and kept chewing.

"*Faster! Faster!*" the pumpkin heads ordered.

"Please—!" Tabby begged, with a mouthful of red liquorice. "We can't—"

"*Faster! Eat! Eat!*"

I shoved an entire chocolate bar into my mouth and struggled to chew. I saw Walker pawing through his bag, looking for something he could eat quickly.

"*Faster! Eat!*" the fiery heads demanded, floating over us. "*Eat! Eat!*"

Lee choked down his fourth Musketeer bar.

He grabbed a Milky Way and started to unwrap it.

"I—I'm going to be sick!" Tabby declared.

"*Faster! Faster!*" came the raspy command.

"No. Really. I feel sick!" she cried.

"*Eat more! Eat—faster!*"

Lee started to choke. A gob of toffee shot out of his mouth. Tabby slapped him on the back until he stopped coughing.

"*More! Faster!*" the pumpkin heads ordered.

"I—I can't!" Lee cried in a hoarse whisper.

The creatures leaned over him, angry flames shooting from their eyes.

Lee grabbed a Crunch bar, tore off the wrapper, and bit into it.

All four of us huddled there on the kerb, gobbling down sweets. Chewing as fast as we could. Forcing it down, then shoving in some more.

Trembling. Frightened. Feeling sick.

We had no idea that the biggest horror was still to come.

"I . . . can't . . . eat . . . any more," Tabby choked out.

We had been stuffing ourselves with sweets for several minutes. Tabby had chocolate running down her chin. And I saw chocolate stuck in the tangles of her blonde hair.

Lee was bent over the grass. He held his stomach and groaned. "I don't feel very well," he murmured. He let out a long, loud burp. And groaned again.

"I never want to see another chocolate bar in my life," Walker whispered to me.

I tried to reply. But my mouth was full.

"*More houses!*" one of the pumpkin heads ordered.

"*More houses! More trick-or-treating!*"

"No—please!" Tabby begged.

Bent over on the grass, Lee let out another long burp.

345

"It's almost midnight!" Tabby protested. "We have to go home!"

"*There are many houses to go,*" a pumpkin head told her, narrowing its fiery eyes. "*Houses for ever. Trick-or-treat for ever!*"

"But we feel sick!" Lee moaned, holding his stomach. "We can't do any more houses tonight!"

"Everyone has gone to sleep," Walker told the pumpkin heads. "No one will answer the door this late."

"*They WILL in this neighbourhood!*" the pumpkin head replied.

"*No problem in THIS neighbourhood,*" the other creature agreed. "*In this neighbourhood, you can trick-or-treat FOR EVER!*"

"But—but—but—!" I sputtered.

I knew it was no use. The fiery creatures were going to force us to keep going. They weren't going to listen to our complaints.

And they weren't going to let us go home.

"*More houses! More! Trick-or-treat for ever!*"

Tabby helped Lee to his feet. She picked up his trick-or-treat bag and placed it in his hand. Then she brushed her hair out of her face and picked up her own bag.

The four of us trooped across the street, dragging the bags beside us. The night air had grown cold and heavy. A strong breeze rattled the trees and sent brown leaves scuttling past our feet.

"Our parents must be so worried," Lee murmured. "It's really late."

"They *should* be worried!" Tabby declared in a trembling voice. "We may never see them again."

The porch light at the first house was still on. The pumpkin heads forced us on to the porch.

"It's too late to trick-or-treat," Lee protested.

But we had no choice. I rang the bell.

We waited. Shivering. Feeling heavy and sick from all the sweets we had forced down.

Slowly, the front door opened.

And we all gasped in shock.

"Ohhh!" A low cry escaped Walker's throat.

Lee jumped off the porch.

I stared at the creature in the yellow porch light. A woman. A woman with a grinning jack-o'-lantern head.

"Trick or treat?" she asked, turning her jagged smile on us. Orange flames danced and flickered inside her head.

"Uh—uh—uh—" Walker hopped off the porch and stumbled into Lee.

I stared at the grinning pumpkin head. *This is a nightmare!* I told myself. *A living nightmare!*

The woman dropped some sweets into my bag. I didn't even see what they were. I couldn't take my eyes off her pumpkin head.

"Are you—?" I started to ask.

But she closed the front door before I could get the words out.

"*More houses!*" the pumpkin heads commanded. "*More trick-or-treating!*"

We dragged ourselves to the next little house. The door swung open as we climbed on to the front doorstep.

And we stared at *another* pumpkin-head creature.

This one wore jeans and a maroon sweatshirt. The flames hissed and crackled behind his eyes and mouth. Two wide, crooked teeth were carved into his mouth—one on top, one below—giving him a silly expression.

But my friends and I were too terrified to laugh.

At the next house, we were greeted by two jack-o'-lantern creatures. We crossed the street and found another fiery-headed creature waiting for us at the next house.

Where *are* we? I wondered.

What *is* this strange neighbourhood?

The two pumpkin heads forced us on to the next block. The houses here all had jack-o'-lantern creatures living in them.

At the end of the block, Tabby set down her trick-or-treat bag and turned to face the pumpkin heads. "Please—let us stop!" she begged. "Please!"

"We can't do any more houses!" Lee exclaimed weakly. "I—I'm so tired. And I really feel sick."

"Please—?" Walker pleaded. "Please—?"

"I can't do another house. I really can't," Tabby said, shaking her head. "I'm so

349

frightened. Those creatures ... in every house ..." She uttered a sob and her voice trailed off.

Lee crossed his arms over the front of his striped costume. "I'm not taking another step," he insisted. "I don't care what you do. I'm not moving."

"Me neither," Tabby agreed, stepping close beside him.

The two pumpkin heads didn't reply. Instead, they rose up high in the air.

I took a step back as their triangle eyes bulged wide and their mouths stretched open. Bright orange flames flew from their eyes.

And then their mouths stretched even wider. And they both let out high wails. The shrill sound rose and fell through the heavy night air. Rose and fell, like police sirens.

The pumpkin heads tilted back until their flames shot straight up to the sky. And their siren wails grew louder. Louder. Until I had to hold my hands over my ears.

I saw a flash of light. And turned to see another pumpkin head floating towards us from across the street.

"Oh!" I uttered a hoarse cry as two more pumpkin-head creatures hurried out of their houses.

And then two more. And another creature. And another.

All down the block, doors flew open.

Creatures floated out. Floated towards us. Hissing and wailing.

Flickering, dancing flames shot out from their jack-o'-lantern eyes and mouths, sending orange light into the black sky. They floated and bobbed down the street, across the dark lawns, wailing like sirens, hissing like snakes.

Closer. Closer.

Dozens of them. Dozens and dozens.

Walker, Tabby, Lee and I pressed close together in the middle of the street as the pumpkin-head creatures drew near.

They formed a circle round us. A circle of grinning, fiery jack-o'-lantern faces over dark-robed bodies.

The circle of creatures spun round us slowly. And as they spun, their heads bobbed and tilted on their shoulders.

Slowly, slowly, they spun round us. And then they began to chant in their hoarse, crackly voices:

"Trick or treat! Trick or treat! Trick or treat!"

"What do they want?" Tabby cried. "What are they going to do?"

I didn't have a chance to answer her.

Four creatures stepped quickly into the middle of the circle.

And when I saw what they carried in their hands, I started to scream.

"*Trick or treat! Trick or treat! Trick or treat!*"

My scream drowned out the chanting pumpkin heads.

And as the four creatures stepped forward, the chanting stopped. Their jack-o'-lantern heads bobbed on their shoulders. Their ragged smiles grew wider as they came near.

They held their hands waist high. In their hands, they each held a pumpkin head.

Four extra pumpkin heads!

"Oh, no!" Lee cried out when he saw them.

Tabby grabbed Lee's arm in terror. "What are they going to do with those heads?"

Bright yellow flames flickered from the eyes and grinning mouths of the four extra heads.

"*These are for you!*" a pumpkin head announced in a voice that sounded like sharp pieces of gravel being rubbed together.

"Ohhh!" A low moan escaped my throat.

I stared at the empty heads, stared at their fiery eyes, their ugly grins.

"These are for you," the pumpkin head repeated, stepping closer. *"These will be your new heads!"*

"No! You can't! You *can't*!" Tabby screamed. "You—"

Her cry was cut off as one of the creatures raised a pumpkin head over her. It had a hole cut in the bottom. The creature slammed the pumpkin head over Tabby's head.

Lee tried to run.

But a creature moved quickly to block his way—and then slammed a pumpkin head on to Lee's head.

I stumbled back, my mouth open in amazement.

Hands pressed helplessly against the sides of their pumpkin heads, Tabby and Lee ran down the street. Ran blindly. Ran screaming. Screaming into the darkness.

And then the creatures turned to Walker and me. And raised the empty pumpkin heads high.

"Please—!" I begged. "Please—no!"

"Please—!" I cried. "Please don't give me a pumpkin head!"

"Please—" Walker joined in.

And then we both burst out laughing.

The two creatures set the empty pumpkin heads down on the ground. And then their own pumpkin heads started to change. The flames died out. The heads began to shrink. And change shape.

A few seconds later, Shane and Shana had their own heads back.

And then all four of us started to laugh. We hugged each other and spun round. We danced wildly, crazily, up and down the street. We tossed back our heads and laughed at the moon and stars. Laughed till it hurt.

"It worked, guys!" I exclaimed when we finally stopped celebrating. "It worked! It worked! We really scared Tabby and Lee this time!"

"They'll be scared for the rest of their lives!"

Walker declared. He slapped Shane on the back. Then he danced another happy dance, waving his hands gleefully above his head.

"We did it! We did it!" I chanted joyfully. "We really scared them! We finally scared them!"

"That was so much fun!" Walker exclaimed. "And so easy!"

I stepped up to Shane and Shana and hugged them both. "Of course," I exclaimed, "it helps to have two aliens from another planet as friends!"

"Whoa! Take it easy!" Shane warned, lowering his voice. He glanced around nervously.

"We don't want any strangers to know that we're not from Earth," Shana said.

"I know, I know!" I replied. "That's why we didn't use your weird powers to scare Tabby and Lee before."

"This year, we were desperate!" Walker declared.

"But we've got to be very careful," Shana said.

Shane rose up and turned to all the other pumpkin-head creatures who were still circling us. "Thanks for your help, brothers and sisters!" Shane called to them. "You'd better hurry home before anyone sees that we have invaded this whole neighbourhood!"

Waving and laughing, murmuring happily to each other, the other pumpkin heads hurried back to their houses. In a few seconds, the street stood empty again—except for us four friends.

We started walking down the middle of the street, making our way home. Walker and I dragged our heavy trick-or-treat bags beside us.

Walker turned to Shane and Shana. A smile spread over his face. "When do you think Tabby and Lee will discover they can just pull off their pumpkin heads?" Walker asked.

"Maybe never!" Shana replied.

And we all started laughing all over again.

We didn't stop until we reached the bottom of my driveway.

"Thanks again," I told Shane and Shana. "You guys were great."

"You were greater than great! You were awesome!" Walker declared. "A couple of times, you even scared *me*! And I knew it was you!"

"And do you know what else is great about having aliens from another planet as friends?" I said. "You two don't eat sweets."

"That's right," Shane and Shana agreed.

"That means Walker and I get to keep it all!" I exclaimed, laughing.

I suddenly had a serious thought. I stopped laughing. "You know, I've never *seen* you two eat," I told the two aliens. "What *do* you eat?"

Shana reached out and pinched my arm. "You're still really bony, Drew," she replied. "You'll find out what Shane and I eat when you fill out a bit."

"Yeah," Shane chimed in. "People from our

planet only like to eat very plump adults. So you don't have to worry for now."

My mouth dropped open. "Hey—you're kidding, right?" I demanded. "Shane? Shana? You're not serious—right? That's a joke. Right? *Right?*"

Are You Ready For
2000 Times
The Scare ...?

Bride of the Living Dummy

"Jillian — what are you *doing*?"

I heard my sister's squeaky voice from my bedroom doorway. I dropped another dead fly into the glass cage. Petey's pointed pink tongue shot out and lapped it up.

"Mmmmm. Juicy fly meat," I murmured to him. "Nice and rare."

"What are you doing?" Katie repeated.

I turned to the door. "I'm practising the violin," I told her.

Katie made a disgusted face. "No, you're not. You're feeding that lizard."

"Duh," I replied, rolling my eyes. I held up a dead fly. "Want a snack? Yum, yum."

"That lizard is gross," she moaned.

"I like him," I insisted. I reached into the cage and tickled Petey under his flat, leathery chin. "It's late. Why are you still up?" I asked my sister.

She yawned. "I'm not tired," she replied.

Amanda, Katie's twin, stepped into the room. "I'm not tired, either," she declared. "And neither is Mary-Ellen. Mary-Ellen wants us to stay up till midnight!"

I groaned. "Get Mary-Ellen out of my room, please," I said through gritted teeth.

"Mary-Ellen can go wherever she wants!" Amanda insisted.

"Mary-Ellen doesn't like you, Jillian," Katie added with a sneer. "She hates you and she hates your lizard!"

"Well, I hate Mary-Ellen!" I cried. "Get her out of my room!"

I know, I know. I was being as babyish as my six-year-old sisters. But I can't help it. I really do hate Mary-Ellen.

Ever since Dad brought Mary-Ellen home, life here at the Zinman house has been difficult.

Mary-Ellen is a huge doll, almost as tall as the twins. She has frizzy brown hair made out of mop yarn. A red, heart-shaped mouth twisted up in a sick grin. Strange violet-coloured glass eyes. And ugly blood-red circles painted on her round cheeks.

The doll is a *horror* — but the girls treat her as a third sister. They dress up the doll in their clothes. They talk to her. They sing to her. They pretend to feed her. And they drag her every-where they go.

They are much nicer to Mary-Ellen than they

are to me. At night, I plan horrible things I'm going to do to that disgusting doll.

Amanda slung the big doll over her shoulder. "Mary-Ellen says we can stay up till midnight," she told me.

I slipped another juicy fly into Petey's open mouth. "I don't think Mum and Dad care what a big, ugly doll says," I replied.

The girls turned and started to leave. "You'll be sorry," Katie warned me. "You'll be sorry you were nasty to Mary-Ellen."

"Mary-Ellen says you'll be sorry," Amanda added. The doll's big head bounced on her shoulder as she walked out of the room.

I slammed the door shut and let out a long sigh. Why do six-year-olds have to be so annoying?

I finished feeding Petey. Then I called a few friends and talked for a while, trying to make plans for the weekend.

I fell asleep around eleven-thirty. I dreamed about my friend Harrison Cohen. I dreamed that he and I could fly. We were flying over our school, and all our friends were amazed.

A sharp *CLICK* pulled me from my dream.

I woke up with a startled gasp. And squinted into the darkness of my room.

I heard another metallic *CLICK*. And then a sharp scraping sound.

A silvery blade flashed in the darkness.

Huh? A blade?
What's going on? I wondered.
I tried to move. Too late.
The blade swooped down to my throat — and
I started to scream.

I shot out both hands. I tried to grab the blade. Push it away.

I heard a soft giggle.

The bedside light flickered on.

"Huh?" I let out a shocked cry as I stared at my sisters' grinning faces.

Katie held a pair of long metal scissors in her hand. Her smile faded. "You ruined our surprise," she moaned.

"Huh? Surprise?" My heart pounded in my chest. "What are you *doing* in here?" I cried breathlessly.

"We wanted to surprise you," Katie replied. "We wanted to give you a haircut."

My mouth dropped open — but no sound came out. I was too horrified to speak.

"A *haircut*?" I finally choked out. "A *haircut*?"

"Why did you have to wake up?" Amanda cried. "You ruined everything!"

"I — I'll ruin *you*!" I cried. With a furious

shriek, I grabbed the scissors from Katie's hand.

The girls are always playing horrid tricks on me. But never anything as horrible as this. "Whatever gave you the idea —?" I sputtered.

"Mary-Ellen said you need a haircut," Katie replied, tugging my hair. "It was Mary-Ellen's idea."

I angrily shoved her hand away. "Get . . . out . . . of . . . my . . . room," I said through gritted teeth. "I will pay you back for this. I promise I will pay you back."

They both sighed and turned to leave.

"Know what I'm going to do?" I called after them. "I'm going to give *Mary-Ellen* a haircut. I'm going to *cut off her head!*"

"Mary-Ellen heard that," Katie replied.

"You'll be sorry," Amanda added.

They slipped back to their room down the hall. It took me hours to get back to sleep. "Maybe I *will* cut the doll's head off," I told myself. "It certainly would improve her looks. . ."

On Saturday afternoon, I was up in my room, waiting for my friend Harrison to show up. Bright sunlight streamed in through the open window. A pretty autumn day.

"Jillian — it's time to go!" I heard Amanda call from out in the hall.

"Yes! Time to go! Time to go!" Katie and Amanda began to chant. "Time to go! Time to go!"

Why do six-year-olds like to chant everything?

"Hey — give me a break!" I held my hands over my ears.

I ignored their cries and gazed into the mirror. I have straight black hair and round green eyes. I'm tall and very thin. I'm the tallest girl in the sixth grade. Sometimes Dad calls me Noodle because I'm so thin and straight.

Guess how much I like that.

The twins are tall and thin and dark-haired too. Katie pulls her hair back in a pony-tail. Amanda usually lets her hair hang over her shoulders.

But I still have trouble telling them apart. Until they talk. Katie is the one with the squeaky voice. She is the crazy one. She is always wired!

Amanda is usually a lot cooler, a lot calmer, a lot quieter and more thoughtful.

Except for now. They were both tugging at me, pulling me to the door, chanting, "Time to go! Time to go!"

"Go where?" I cried.

Mum swept into the room, carrying a pile of clean T-shirts. She set them down on my bed, then made a face at Petey. She hates him too.

"Jillian, have you forgotten about taking your sisters to the Little Theatre?" she demanded.

"Oh, no!" I wailed. "I *had* forgotten!"

Weeks ago, I'd promised the twins I'd take them to see the ventriloquist show at the Saturday matinee.

"You *have* to take us!" Katie squeaked. She tugged my arm so hard, my shoulder cracked.

"You *have* to!" Amanda repeated.

"But I'm meeting Harrison," I protested to Mum. Harrison lives down the block. We've been best friends ever since I made him eat a whole bowl of mud in first grade.

That was five years ago. So far, Harrison hasn't done anything to pay me back. I think he's waiting for the right moment.

Mum squinted hard at me. Her no-nonsense look. "You promised them, and you are taking them — now!" she ordered.

The twins exploded in a deafening cheer.

"Take Harrison with you," Mum added. "I'm sure he'll enjoy the show."

Yeah. Of course. About as much as eating mud.

Mum squinted at me even harder. "Jillian, you want to make money entertaining kids at birthday parties — right?"

"Right," I replied.

"So maybe you'll get some good ideas at this show," Mum said.

I groaned. "Mum — I want to be a clown. Not a stupid ventriloquist."

Mum leant close to me. "You promised them," she whispered.

"Okay, okay. We're going," I said.

The twins cheered again.

"Actually, Harrison likes this kind of stuff," I added. "He'll probably think the show is amazing."

"If Harrison is coming, then Mary-Ellen has to come too!" Katie cried.

"Yes!" Amanda agreed. "Mary-Ellen wants to see the ventriloquist."

"No way!" I protested. "There's no way I'm taking that big, ugly monster!"

Amanda disappeared across the hall into the room she and Katie share. A few seconds later, she was back, dragging the big doll. "Mary-Ellen says she has to come with us!"

"But — but —" I sputtered. "She's too big. I'll have to buy a ticket for her. She will have to have her own seat!"

"I'll hold her in my lap!" Katie cried.

"No. *I'll* hold her!" Amanda insisted.

"I'm not taking her," I insisted. I glanced at the clock on the mantelpiece. "Put the doll down and let's go," I said. I picked up my bag.

Amanda didn't move. She hugged the big doll. "I'm not going unless Mary-Ellen goes too!"

"I'm not going, either," Katie croaked in her scratchy voice.

"Okay, okay," I sighed. I could see that I wasn't going to win this argument. "You can bring the doll."

They both cheered. They love winning. And since they are spoilt brats and almost always win, they have a lot of practice cheering.

A deafening sound — a shrill whine — blared through the room. "What is *that*?" I cried.

"You know. It's your dad," Mum replied.

Another shrill whine made me cover my ears.

"He's down in his workshop." Mum sighed. "Still sawing away at that coffee table."

"He's been building that table for six months," I said.

"I'm sure it will be beautiful when it's finished." Mum glanced at the clock. "You're really going to be late."

"Come on, you two," I said. "Let's go and see this show."

"Mary-Ellen too!" Katie reminded me.

"I know. I know," I groaned.

She swung the big doll around. Her heavy plastic hand slapped me in the face. "Hey —!" I cried out angrily.

"Mary-Ellen did it. Not me!" Katie insisted. She stuck out her tongue at me.

Harrison was just walking up the driveway. He's very big. Not chubby. Just *biiig*. Big head, big chest, big, muscular arms and legs. He has a round face, dark, serious eyes and short dark hair.

"What's up?" he called.

"We're going to a ventriloquist show," I told him. "All of us."

"Cool," he replied.

I knew he'd like it.

I thought I'd be bored to tears.

And I was right about that. But here's what I didn't know.

I didn't know this show would ruin our lives.

Look for more books in the Goosebumps Series 2000
by R.L. Stine:

1 Cry of the Cat
2 Bride of the Living Dummy
3 Creature Teacher
4 Invasion of the Body Squeezers Part 1
5 Invasion of the Body Squeezers Part 2
6 I Am Your Evil Twin
7 Revenge R Us
8 Fright Camp
9 Are You Terrified Yet?
10 Headless Halloween
11 Attack of the Graveyard Ghouls
12 Brain Juice
13 Return to HorrorLand
14 Jekyll and Heidi
15 Scream School
16 The Mummy Walks
17 The Werewolf in the Living Room
18 Horrors of the Black Ring
19 Return to Ghost Camp

And coming soon:

20 Be Afraid—Be Very Afraid!